CUPID CALAMITY

KELLY KAY
EVIE ALEXANDER

EMLIN
PRESS

First Published in Great Britain 2022 by Emlin Press in conjunction with Decorated Cast, LLC.

ISBN (eBook) 978-1-914473-08-1

ISBN (Print) 978-1-914473-09-8

A CIP catalogue record for this book is available from the British Library.

www.emlinpress.com

EMLIN
PRESS

*To the readers who have found us
and changed our lives.
And the ones just finding us, welcome.*

Also

*To The Smut Hut and The Hub.
Places that allow for creation. And laughs.
Lots of laughs.*

NOTE TO READERS

Hi. Hello. Welcome to

EVIE & KELLY'S HOLIDAY DISASTERS

Madness, mirth and steam. Hilarious side by side novellas with interconnected characters focusing on one holiday and one trope at a time.

Our Holiday Disasters series was developed over many Zoom calls as we laughed and puzzled over how to work together. Our writing styles may be different but our humor/humour complements each other very well.

Kelly conceived the concept of Holiday Disasters during a wine-induced fever dream. Evie agreed to it in the midst of a chocolate-induced sugar high.

6 Stories
6 Happily Ever Afters

3 Holidays
3 Tropes
2 Time Zones
2 Authors
Multiple disasters
And 1 Asshole Monkey

Volume One

Featuring four new characters and two plucked from our already existing universes trapped in an airport lounge as they forge unlikely friendships. Each novella focuses on one of these characters and their happily ever after. The sextet stays in touch throughout the year and the series.

Volume One Holidays & Tropes
Valentine's Day - Insta-Love
Fourth of July - Friends to Lovers
Christmas - A visit with old friends from our respective writing universes

We hope you enjoy reading these as much as we enjoyed writing them. See you on the other side.

Much love,
    Evie & Kelly

❧ I ❧
ANIMAL ATTRACTION

By
Evie Alexander

PROLOGUE

February 12 – Chicago, IL
United Lounge, O'Hare airport
11:07 a.m. US CST

The noise crashed through the glass walls of the airport lounge with such force that Ben felt his chest reverberate. Then the lights cut out.

'What the fuck?' yelled an American woman.

Two enormous fellow passengers ran like Special Forces gorillas, one towards the window, the other towards the door. Ben caught the eye of a man in a tailored three-piece suit sitting across from him in another bank of chairs and they shrugged at each other. The man had a British passport resting on top of a leather briefcase.

The speaker above Ben's head turned on with a screech of feedback.

'Please remain seated and calm—'

'Like fuck I will.' The brash, dark-haired American woman strode towards the welcome desk, where one of the great apes was talking to the lounge attendant. Ben swivelled in his seat to watch the show. The woman tapped the big man on the shoulder like a woodpecker attacking a concrete pole.

'Yo, Bigfoot. I got this.'

The man-mountain turned and looked down at her, raising his eyebrows.

'Bigfoot?' His voice a low rumble of disdain and annoyance.

'You're a Sasquatch, no?'

Ben grinned. Bigfoot/Sasquatch was also a Brit. So with him and fancy-suit guy, that made three. The only other passengers in the lounge were the other gorilla, now walking back from the glass like he'd misplaced his grenade launcher, the loud dark-haired woman arguing with Bigfoot, and a small blonde, frantically scrolling her mobile for answers.

'Do you know how long the flight to Edinburgh will be delayed?' Bigfoot asked the attendant.

She ignored him and turned her back to answer a phone.

The speaker shrieked back to life and another voice echoed from the ceiling.

'Ladies and gentlemen, please remain calm. Lightning has struck a transformer in the terminal and we are initiating emergency procedures. All facilities are being locked down while we resolve this situation and wait for full power to be restored. Generator lights will activate momentarily. You must remain in your seat and await further instruction. All flights departing Chicago O'Hare will be delayed. You will be kept up to date.'

Ben sighed and ran his hands through his hair. After many years he was finally leaving the States, but it seemed his adopted country didn't want to let him go.

The lounge attendant scurried to the door, made an escape

and locked it behind her. The loud woman let out a torrent of abuse as she banged on the wood, then turned to face the room and let out a sigh.

'Who wants to get wasted? Or is it pissed?' Her attention was directed to the end of the lounge where Ben was seated. She didn't wait for a response. She looked pointedly at each of them, like a preschool teacher doing roll call. 'Okay, Cranky Bigfoot, Farm boy, Hugh Grant, Prince William and Cheerleader, gather round. Let's turn this shit into a show.'

'Cheerleader?' piped up the pretty blonde. 'Then who are you?'

'I'm Tabi Aganos. Come on, there's only the six of us and a lot of time on our hands. I'm not good at bored. But I can get us provisions.'

She leaned over the recently abandoned bar. After some more cursing, she flipped back over, holding wine, cheese and chocolate. She put them down and gestured for everyone to join her.

Ben caught the eye of the bloke in the fancy suit and they shrugged at each other as if to say 'what the hell, why not?' They both ambled over.

'I'm Tristan,' said suit guy, extending his hand to Tabi. 'Are you a thief?'

'Today I am,' Tabi grinned. 'And funnily enough, this is from my winery, Prohibition Vineyards. I was on a sales call here in O'Hare signing the contract for this lounge to carry our hooch. Gather round children and taste some fine-ass wine.'

'I'm Ben.'

'Sabrina,' said the blonde. 'And I'm not a cheerleader. Not even close.'

Tabi grinned at her. 'By the end of this evening we're going to know more about you than even your own mother.'

Sabrina flicked her hand at the comment. 'Wouldn't be hard.'

'Hey, everyone, nice to meet you,' said the blond farm boy crossed with a linebacker. He had the most open and honest smile Ben had seen in a long time. 'I'm Jonathan.'

'Hey, Jonathan,' replied Tabi. 'Who's your surly older brother?'

'No idea,' he said cheerfully, before extending his arm to Bigfoot. 'I'm Jonathan.'

There was a pause that nearly became embarrassing, before Bigfoot grasped the concept of etiquette, closely followed by Jonathan's hand.

'I'm Rory,' he replied. 'And I don't drink.'

Tabi gave Rory a round of applause and he scowled at her. She winked, opened the first bottle of wine, then waved a wheel of cheese and a bar of chocolate in his face. He growled.

'Right then, Jonathan, Sabrina, Tristan and Ben. Let's get drunk and spill all our secrets. Kilt, you're just going to have to do it high on fermented milk products and cocoa.'

Rory raised an eyebrow. 'Kilt?' he asked.

Tabi shrugged. 'You're flying to Edinburgh. Scottish: grumpy, bagpipes, kilt.'

Rory held up his massive hand, counting on his fingers. 'American: loud, fanny pack, cheeseburgers.'

Tabi high-fived him. 'Fuck, yeah!' she yelled.

Ben grinned. Suddenly the delay didn't seem so bad. This would be an impromptu party celebrating his last night in America. The closing of a chapter in his life before the start of a new one. He'd have a couple of drinks with some random strangers, then he'd leave for the UK and the most important meeting of his life.

'No, you carry a handkerchief and slap it against someone else's when you dance. Or sticks. Actually, usually sticks. The bells are on your knees. And you've gorra have a beard. So you'd be no good,' Ben slurred as he tried to explain Morris dancing to Jonathan. Bloody fucking hell he was wasted.

'And this is traditional?' Jonathan asked.

'Yeah, and cider. My dad makes scrumpy. You can drink it or use it to kill rats.'

Ben squinted to bring Jonathan's face back into focus. 'Why aren't you drunk? I'm pissed as a fart.'

Jonathan smiled. 'What else is in Somerset?'

'Sheep. And lots of gorges. They're gorgeous.' Ben giggled at his own joke. 'They're *gorgeous*,' he repeated between snorts.

'What's gorgeous?' yelled Tabi.

'Sheep,' replied Jonathan. 'Apparently this Somerset place is full of them.'

'And that's why you're going back? For sheep?' she asked incredulously.

The rest of the group started laughing, and even Rory managed a chuckle. Ben shook his head and tried to remember exactly why he was leaving America.

Oh fuck. Yes. *That*. He put his glass of wine down. He could not be hungover. He wouldn't get a second chance to make a first impression.

Tabi waved her phone at him. 'We've got your number now, Ben. You need to send us a picture of you with your favourite sheep.'

He grinned at his new friends. It could be the wine, the company, or the promise of the future, but right now he felt he could do this. Everything in Somerset was going to be perfect.

February 14 – Somerset

The noise crashed through the walls of the office with such force that the half-chewed biros rattled in their dusty mugs and the monitor of Laurie's ancient computer flickered. Her heart spiked but she didn't move. She waited. Surely today, of all days, someone else would step up? Her fingers twitched, suspended over the keys. The sounds from the warehouse next door changed to shouting. She glanced up. Everyone was looking at her. *Fine.* She pushed back her chair, stood and stalked to the door, metaphorically rolling up her sleeves to deal with the inevitable shitstorm awaiting her on the other side.

She was not disappointed.

The warehouse of Somerset Snax was usually in order, Laurie made sure of it. But now it was in chaos. A pallet had fallen off a forklift, discharging five thousand four hundred and forty-six cans of Blackcurrant Bliss to go off like overly tired toddlers at soft play. The concrete floor was a fizzing purple sea of stickiness, and standing in the middle of it all, looking at the ceiling, were three muppets loosely disguised as men.

Laurie didn't need to be Miss Marple to work out what had happened. One of them – she guessed Kevin due to the colour of his cheeks – had backed the forklift into one of the enormous shelving units, dented one of the supporting uprights and got wedged. Knowing him, he then panicked, and with his limited cognitive function, tipped the pallet of drinks onto the floor as he tried to get out. Now, one of the high shelves was leaning ominously. It was not only a god-awful mess, but a fatal accident waiting to happen.

Despite all the words fighting to exit her mouth, Laurie was at work. She was a professional in an increasingly unprofessional environment, so reluctantly pushed them into the overstuffed room of her mind marked 'things I want to say to my fuckwit colleagues', locked the door and forced a smile.

'Okay. Barry, how about you get a bucket, empty out any half-full cans, then put them in the recycling? Kevin, why don't you get the mop and start clearing this up? Trevor, can you pick the pallet back up and take it out into the yard? I'll find the hazard tape and start filing the accident report.'

Barry and Kevin moved off, but Trevor's feet had stopped working. Laurie watched him looking between the forklift and the damaged shelving above, as he rubbed a dirty hand through the remains of his hair. She gritted her teeth.

'You help the guys instead, eh?'

He nodded and scurried off; the final rat leaving the sinking ship.

Laurie picked her way gingerly across the floor and climbed up into the cab. It had been designed for a man, so her six-foot frame could be accommodated. But forklift drivers didn't usually operate them wearing tight pencil skirts and heels. Laurie foolishly believed if she dressed like she belonged in an office, she wouldn't keep getting called into the warehouse to do other people's jobs. However, once everyone knew she combined loyalty and perfectionism with the inability to say no, they made sure she was driving the good ship Somerset Snax, whilst they hung out on the back deck drinking beer.

With practiced skill, she got the pallet back on the fork-lift and drove it into the yard. The icy rain was biting, sending sharp shocks across the back of her hands and slapping into her white shirt. February was always a cruel month on the Mendips, but today was especially bitter. She knew she should go back into the warmth of the office, but also knew if she didn't chivvy the men along they wouldn't make the delivery schedule for that afternoon. After Christmas, this was the busiest weekend of the year, and last-minute orders had been coming in all day. So, as ever, she led by example, doing a job she wasn't contracted or paid to do, whilst Barry, Kevin and Trevor *helped* by standing too close and staring at her large breasts, as her top turned translucent in the rain.

An hour later, Laurie was in the ladies, holding her sodden shirt against the ineffective dryer and trying to avoid the Valentine's day decorations tacked to the low ceiling. The door opened with a squeak and a pretty blonde girl breezed in, gliding under the pink balloons.

'There you are!' she said.

'Hey, Stacie.'

'All sorted?'

Laurie grimaced. 'I've seen worse but it's under control now.'

She tucked her shirt back in and the two women looked at themselves in the mirror. Stacie was Laurie's closest friend at work and the two women could not have been any more different. Stacie was petite, blonde, and bubbly. Laurie was tall and full- figured, with brown skin and curly black hair. Right now, she felt like all the fun had been sucked out of her.

'Sorry I can't celebrate your birthday with you, Laurie. It's just, you know, today is so special to me and Nath.'

Laurie forced another smile and nodded. Valentine's Day was for people like Stacie, not her. Her friend was utterly in love with Nathan, the operations director at Somerset Snax. Laurie hadn't dated anyone since Scott, and had no illusions about love after his prick burst that bubble with a beauty therapist from Shepton Mallet.

'You didn't think of going back to see your family this weekend?' Stacie asked, applying another layer of pink to her lips.

Laurie took off her glasses to clean them, and retreated into a blurry world. Having a birthday on the 14th of February sucked. No one was free, and everywhere was booked or too expensive. She cleared her throat.

'Liverpool's too far for just a couple of nights. And Shelly and Denise said they would take me out.'

Laurie was glad her glasses were off so she couldn't see the look she knew was on Stacie's face. Denise and Shelley worked in payroll at Somerset Snax, were in their late fifties, and had fallen out of love long ago. A night out with them always involved vast quantities of alcohol followed by a diatribe detailing the shortcomings of fifty per cent of the population.

'That'll be nice,' Stacie finally managed.

Laurie put her glasses back on and squared her shoulders. She could do this. Turning thirty wasn't that big a deal.

Stacie took her hand and pulled her out of the bathroom.

'Come on, Laurie, let's get back to work.'

Laurie took a breath in and dredged up another smile for her friend. She would get through work and enjoy a night out.

Following Stacie into the office, Laurie stopped in surprise.

'Happy birthday to you, happy birthday to you, happy birthday dear Laurie... Happy birthday to you.'

Everyone was there. They were singing and actually celebrating her birthday. Like a dog begging for emotional scraps, Laurie forgot how they normally treated her and her heart swelled. She smiled as Nathan brought forward a large, rectangular cake. It was a mountain of pink and white frosting, with the word 'CONGRATULATIONS' piped on top. Despite how grotesque it looked, her mouth watered. *Please let it be chocolate.*

'Happy birthday, Laurie,' said Nathan, handing her a knife. 'Want to cut it?'

She beamed down at his pink perspiring face. 'Thank you, Nathan, and thank you, everyone. This is really lovely.'

There was silence as she held the knife over the frosting. What should she wish for? Her hand hovered. It needed to be right.

'Come on, Laurie,' urged Nathan, jigging up and down next to her impatiently.

She closed her eyes and plunged the knife down. *I want more out of my life.*

The knife was taken from her hand, as she was jostled out of the way.

'Right, everyone, who wants a piece?' asked Nathan. He magnanimously handed her the first slice. Red velvet. Stacie's favourite. Had she ordered it? Nathan carefully cut one of the corners and presented it to Stacie who squealed with excitement. Okay, so not her then. Laurie looked around the room, but no one had a smug look that said 'look at me, I did this.' She shrugged and ate her slice. *Just be grateful they remembered.*

A high-pitched shriek rent the air and Laurie looked up in panic. Stacie was holding a glob of chewed cake in her palm.

Had she lost a tooth? She rushed to her friend. 'You okay, Stace?'

'Laurie, get out of the way.' Nathan shoved her aside and she stumbled into a desk, cake dropping out of her grasp onto her skirt. Stacie was now crying, and Nathan was on one knee. 'Stacie Tanner,' he declared loudly.

'Yes, yes, yes, yes, yes!' screamed Stacie, as all the other women in the office bar Laurie started squealing with excitement.

Nathan bellowed over the racket, 'Will you marry me?'

2

L aurie may not have known their destination for the evening, but she knew without asking that she would be the designated driver. She didn't have anything against drinking; in fact, she loved anything fizzy and alcoholic. But at her first office party at Somerset Snax, she knew within ten minutes if someone didn't stay sober, it was only a matter of time before Nathan and Stacie broke the photocopier trying to have sex on it, and the forklifts were drag racing through Downhead. After taking on the role of parent, health and safety enforcer, and police liaison officer, her colleagues had assumed she didn't drink. They subsequently took advantage of her outside work hours as well, and she often wondered if the only reason she had a social life at all was because she provided a free taxi service. She could have indulged at home, in the flat she once shared with Scott. However, drinking by herself seemed like the first step towards owning twenty cats, feeding pigeons at the park, and muttering to herself at the bus stop.

Her first pickup, Denise, bustled out of her house in a

cloud of curse words and chemicals. Her hair was an immaculate helmet of lacquer and her make-up artfully applied. A miasma of perfume clung to her clothes. She was dressed to take on Friday night and win.

'Boring fucking bastard,' she exhaled, as she flumped herself into the passenger seat. 'I spent the best years of my life supporting him, raising the kids, and now I want to live a little.' She leaned forward to flick on the radio, tuning it to Kiss FM. 'It's like he's given up on life already.' She swivelled to look at Laurie. 'You look lush, love. New top?'

Laurie smiled and nodded. She'd found a gold sequinned top online, with a daring V front that emphasised her cleavage. She paired it with a tight black pencil skirt, gold hooped earrings and gold eyeshadow. For the first in a long time she felt confident.

'Well, it'll be slim pickings tonight, but we'll see what we can scrape up for you.'

'I'm not after anyone, you know that.'

'Not even a birthday kiss? Snog a stranger?'

Laurie raised an eyebrow. 'That's not my style.'

'Hmmph. Sometimes you're too hoity-toity for your own good, Laurie.'

Laurie couldn't help a snort of laughter from escaping. 'I'm from Liverpool, Den. I don't think any of us have ever been described as hoity-toity.'

'Well, there's obviously a posh part somewhere up in Scouse land, and you're from it.'

Denise cranked the volume on the radio and sang along to the nineties club tunes, every word on point even if the pitch wasn't. Laurie drove through the dark country roads, enjoying the moment. Ten minutes later they picked up Shelley, who had squeezed into a leopard print dress and was glowing from at least one drink and newly applied fake tan.

She threw herself into the back seat and leaned forward, thrusting a can at Denise. 'Pink G and T.' She turned to Laurie. 'Happy birthday, love. You look gorge.' She took a can out of her bag for herself and clunked it against Denise's.

'Do not spill any of that in my car, ladies,' said Laurie sternly. 'And, Shelley, put your seatbelt on.'

'Yes, Miss,' they replied simultaneously before dissolving into giggles.

Laurie eyeballed Shelley and held back a sigh. 'Okay then, where are we going?'

Shelley's eyes lit up and she bounced up and down so vigorously her breasts nearly escaped from her dress. 'You're going to love me forever and ever and ever, darl.'

Laurie waited patiently for Shelley's excitement to come to the boil.

'Ohmygod I've got us a table at Buttley Manor!'

Huh? 'The safari park?'

'Yesssssss! Come on, Laurie, you must have heard about their new restaurant, Out of Africa?'

Laurie racked her brains. She'd never visited and always tuned out gossip at work. 'Um. I'm not sure.'

'You need to pay attention to the important stuff, Laur. It's super bloody exclusive. Waiting list longer than your dry spell.'

Denise cackled at Shelley's joke, then they both started singing along to the radio with the vocal ability of football supporters:

'*Eeny-weeny, teeny-weeny, shrivelled little short dick man. Don't, don't, don't, don't—*'

'So, how did you get a table?' shouted Laurie.

'I know the owner. Met in the sauna at the golf club,' said Shelley.

'Golf clubs have saunas?'

'This one does. It's got a spa for the bored wives and for

the men when they've spent too much time riding about on golf buggies.'

Laurie grinned. 'And where do you fit into that picture?'

'That's what all the wives are asking,' said Denise, and the two women clunked their cans together and laughed.

THE MENDIPS HAD BEEN DESIGNATED, MANY YEARS AGO, AS an AONB, an Area of Outstanding Natural Beauty. It was a series of limestone hills with lakes, natural springs, dramatic gorges and rocky outcrops. It was sparsely inhabited, but had hundreds of ancient burial mounds dotted around the fields. It was a place of myth and legend, and at night, the darkness could feel overwhelming. As Laurie turned off the main road into the grounds of Buttley Manor, she shrank inwards. Heavily fortified fences were just visible on either side of the endless drive, but she couldn't decide if the dark shapes on the other side were animal, vegetable or mineral. Should she slow down to avoid crashing into a wayward zebra, or speed up in case a hungry lion was on the loose?

Shelley finished her gin and leaned forward between the seats. 'It's owned by Sebastian Ottily-Davenport. He got the place two years ago after his dad was on an illegal hunt and got trampled by elephants.'

'Oh no, that's awful!' Laurie gasped.

'Not really, the elephants were fine, and Seb hated his dad. He got the estate and could do what he liked with it.' Shelley's voice dropped. 'You know, he told me he did it.'

'He did what?'

'He killed his dad!'

'What? How?'

'He told the elephants to do it.'

'Er... How?'

'He can talk to animals. He's a real-life Dr Dolittle. He told me his abilities came after he got lost in the bush as a child and was adopted by a family of monkeys.'

'Adopted? For how long?'

'Only a night. He was retrieved in the morning when his dad and his team rescued him and shot all the monkeys.'

'Holy shit!'

'Yeah, it was the most important moment of his life. Seb told me that day he vowed to avenge his monkey family and create a safari park at Buttley to bring the wonders of Africa to Somerset.'

Laurie didn't know what to say, so kept quiet as they continued down the long drive. In the distance was a stately home, illuminated by colourful floodlights.

'But it's not any old park. Seb encourages visitors to interact with the animals, and he teaches courses on inter-species communication.'

Laurie gripped the steering wheel tighter. She wasn't a fan of animals since being mauled by a Siamese cat as a child. She still had faint scars on her hands and arms, and they prickled if any animal got too close. Even hamsters.

'Interaction?' She could hear how high her voice had become.

'Oh, it's perfectly safe. Seb knows what he's doing. He's even taken me to pet Ryan.'

'Ryan?'

'The lion. Well, one of them anyway. I nearly shat myself.'

Laurie slammed her foot on the brake and Shelley flew forward, getting wedged between the front seats. The car came to a shuddering stop.

'Shelley! This is dangerous! I thought we were going *for* a meal, not to *be* a meal! And I told you to put your seatbelt on!'

Denise was laughing so hard every inhale was a snort.

'Fuck's sake, Laur, it's fine! You're so bloody boring some-times,' Shelley grumbled as she extricated herself. 'The only dangerous animals are the hippos, and they're never let loose. Me and Den'll look after you. Promise.'

Laurie parked at the side of the stately home, alongside a fleet of other cars. Their feet crunched down a gravel walkway towards the old coach house. It was an impressive, two-storey building on one side of a large courtyard, looking down on the stable blocks that flanked the other sides. The enormous old wooden doors were open. Light and chatter spilled out over the small queue of hand-holding couples. Laurie stiffened with the sense of not fitting in. Her height always made her stand out, and tonight it highlighted the fact she was out on Valen-tine's Day partnerless. Shelley grabbed her arm.

'Let's pretend we're a throuple,' she hissed.

'Yes!' agreed Denise. 'Shell and I have been together for years, and you're our unicorn.'

'A *what*?'

'A unicorn. An unthreatening add-on. You're a sexy third wheel.'

Laurie sensed a yawning chasm in her chest, an empty hole where her heart should be. Was this how everyone saw her? Unthreatening? A third wheel? She couldn't even formulate a response because they'd reached the front of the queue. Shelley was talking to a woman with a clipboard in one hand, a walkie-talkie in the other, and an enormous snake wrapped around her neck. Laurie tried to step back, but Denise gripped her arm.

'Party of three. Booked under the name Lawler.'

'Yes, I have you. Clarence will show you to your table.'

A man stepped forward, holding the hand of a chimpanzee, who leered at the three of them, then walked into the main room, beckoning them to follow.

'Ohmygod this is so coooool!' squealed Shelley, as she pulled Laurie forward.

The former coach house was a large, rectangular building. A bar had been built along most of the right-hand side, and the far end was dedicated to an open-plan kitchen area. Two doors on the left were marked as toilets and another, beside the bar, had 'staff' painted on it. Laurie's eyes darted around, her unconscious and conscious minds joining forces to survey the scene for danger (everywhere) and escape routes (not enough). Tables for two filled the space, all populated by couples gazing into each other's eyes and admiring the animals around them. Birds and butterflies flew across the room, monkeys helped serve food, and everything from porcupines to piglets bustled about searching for scraps. It was a Disney cartoon come to life – with more noise and excrement.

They were led to a larger table off to the side near the bar, and Laurie positioned herself with her back to the wall. This definitely didn't feel safe. She fixed her smile on the waiter as he handed them their menus, but couldn't fully concentrate on his description of the specials, as something pink was waving about in her peripheral vision. Denise started honking with laughter, then Shelley joined in.

'I think we've pulled!' screeched Shelley as the waiter dragged the aroused chimp away.

'Oh my lord, I haven't seen anything that funny in years,' said Denise, wiping tears from the corners of her eyes.

3

B y the time their waiter and a less amorous monkey had delivered their drinks and taken their order, Laurie was in full fight or flight mode. She felt unsafe around elderly lap dogs, so being in a room with the cast of *The Jungle Book* was like entering a Darwinian *Hunger Games* armed with only a breadstick. Denise and Shelley had ordered a bottle of Cava to celebrate her birthday. After calculating the alcohol content, her weight, height, the amount of wheat-based products currently lining her stomach, and the most conservative estimation of when she could get the hell out of there, Laurie poured herself a glass.

'Oooh! You go, girl! Finally letting your hair down,' crowed Shelley.

'About time too. You need to live a little,' added Denise. 'Get laid. Our waiter is fit, you should ask him out.'

Laurie nearly choked. 'Den, no! For a start he looks about twelve, and secondly, he's half my height. If we stood next to each other, his head... ' She stopped talking but it was too late.

'Would be the perfect height to suck your tits!'

'Denise!'

Shelley laid her hand on Laurie's arm as Denise cackled into her Cava. 'Laurie, love. You need to put yourself out there. You need to find someone. You're like a fussy ice queen.'

'I am not!'

'Yes, you are,' added Denise. 'When did you last approach a bloke, eh?'

Laurie shuffled through the filing cabinet of her mind, determined to refute them, but came up short. 'Why do I need a man to make me happy? And anyway, you're always going on about how much you hate men.'

'We don't hate *all* men,' said Denise. 'Just Shelley's ex and my useless husband. The rest we only mildly dislike or tolerate. Come on, Laur, ask the waiter out. If you don't then we will. Look, he's coming back with our starters.'

'Denise!' Laurie hissed. 'If you say anything, I'm leaving right now, and I'm not taking you with me. I categorically refuse to go out with anyone younger or smaller than me.'

As they ate their starters, Laurie systematically scanned the room. Before, she'd only noticed the animals, but now she looked at the people. Her fellow diners were instantly dismissed as they were in relationships, but the staff? Maybe if she flirted a bit, gave one of them a fake number, it might get Denise and Shelley off her back. But nobody caught her eye. They looked too young, too nervous or both. She didn't blame them. She wouldn't want to be in charge of any animal, let alone one that could bite your finger off for fun. However, they'd no doubt be just as jumpy around her. She always made men nervous. She tried to hide her intelligence and practised slouching to mask her height, but it was never enough. On some level, they knew her brain was even bigger than her body. So, to compensate they mansplained, made her the butt of their unfunny jokes; they diminished her to elevate themselves.

She was so tired of it. It was easier not to bother interacting with them in the first place.

However, when her gaze reached the bar, it stopped. Sitting on his own, with his back to them, was a man with all his own hair and a very nice-looking suit. Laurie couldn't see his face so took in the details she could account for. She guessed he was waiting for someone and had come on his own. There was a half-empty tumbler next to him and he was looking at his phone. He put it on the bar, turned, and looked out across the room. Laurie's heart jumped. Now side-on, she could see the strong line of his jaw. His skin was pale but his hair was almost black, and even from a few yards away, she could see his eyes were blue. He was—

'Eeek! It's Seb! SEB!!! Over here!'

Shelley's arm was in the air, straining towards the ceiling, her fingertips fluttering for attention like a school kid with an overly full bladder, desperate to be excused. Laurie dragged her attention away from the bar to see a tall, slim man striding across the room, a spider monkey on his shoulder. He looked to be in his late forties, wearing dusty red chinos and a jacket covered in pockets. He had dirty blond hair sticking up in all directions, flushed cheeks, and eyes so wide all the white around the irises was showing.

'Shelley! Oh my dahhhling, you are looking divine. That dress... ' He broke off and mimed biting a chunk out of it, leaving a few drops of spittle on his lower lip. Shelley was on her feet, smoothing her leopard print dress down over her thighs and breathing her breasts up towards his face. He pulled her to his side and growled into her neck.

Shelley giggled with excitement, then shrieked. 'Fuck!' She pulled back with a jerk and Laurie instinctively stood. Shelley's hand came to her ear. 'It bit me!'

The monkey on Seb's shoulder grinned, showing white teeth stained red with blood.

'Shelley, let me look.' Laurie held a napkin to her friend's ear to inspect the damage and sagged with relief. 'It's okay, just a nick.'

Seb held the monkey up to his face. 'Now, Itsy-Bitsy, we know that's not the right way to behave. Don't we?' It chattered with excitement. 'I understand, but you need to talk about these feelings. Talkie, talkie instead of bitey, bitey. Okay?' It cast its eyes down, then started picking through Seb's hair for lice. Seb turned to Shelley. 'Itsy-Bitsy is unfortunately an itsy-bit jealous of you.'

Shelley smiled, folded the bloodied napkin, and put it down on the table. 'Jealous, eh?'

Laurie's heart was racing, her palms clammy. She cleared her throat. 'Mr Ottily-Davenport. My name is Lauren Dover, and I am incredibly concerned about the safety of this event, not to mention the ethics and legality.'

'Are you a member of the local constabulary?' he asked, with a smile so broad he must have known she was not.

'No, however, I am the health and safety officer, and emergency first aid responder at my place of work, and this is dangerous and unethical.'

'Laurie! Shut up!' hissed Shelley.

'This isn't right or fair on the animals, and—'

Seb laughed. 'I can assure you, these animals have a better life than I do.'

Denise grabbed Laurie's hand and pulled her back into her seat. 'Don't worry about her, Mr Otterly-Davidoff, our Laurie's the fun police. When she does a risk assessment, she makes sure there's no risk at all.'

Seb smiled magnanimously down at Laurie. 'I completely understand. The animals can be a little overwhelming to the senses at first, but look around. Isn't everyone having a wonderful time?'

Laurie looked at the rest of the room. Everyone did seem to be enjoying themselves. Was this really what she was? Someone who never took a risk? The *fun police*?

Seb looked at his watch. 'Ladies, cast your eyes over to table eleven. Magic is about to happen.'

Laurie looked over, her eyes making the journey via the bar, where the good-looking man was now drumming his fingers impatiently on the sides of his glass. A gong rang out, and the humans in the room fell silent. Two staff members approached a table in the middle of the room. One held the hand of a chimpanzee, the other carried a small black bird. At the table sat a confused looking woman and a man who looked like he was about to be shot. The man stood with a jerk, then dropped to one knee.

'Woman!' the bird squawked. 'Will you marry me?'

She looked between the bird and her expectant boyfriend, then at the monkey, who thrust an opened ring box towards her.

'Eleanor?'

The penny finally dropped and she squealed, clapping her hands together. 'Yes! I will!' Eleanor's now-fiancé got to his feet and reached to take the ring from the monkey. It pulled the box back. The man hesitated, then tried again. The monkey hissed. The staff member holding the monkey's hand took a treat out of his pocket and bartered it for the box.

'Woman! Will you marry me?' shrieked the bird again.

The animals were quickly led away and Seb clapped enthusiastically, encouraging everyone else to join in.

Shelley dabbed the corners of her eyes. 'That was beautiful.'

'And that's just the beginning! We've got many more to come, including one with Nellie,' said Seb.

'The elephant? That's so adorable!'

'Ladies,' said Seb. 'You must excuse me, I have a meeting outside with my special friends.' He gave them a short bow and walked off.

Laurie's heart was hammering. 'Shelley, Den, I don't feel safe.'

Shelley huffed. 'It's fine. He knows what he's doing. Seriously, you need to lighten up, Laur. Stop being so bloody boring. Take a risk for once in your life.'

Laurie dug her nails into her thighs. She glanced over to the bar. The man put his phone in his pocket and signalled to the barman. *Shit*. He was leaving.

'I do take risks,' she countered. 'I take risks every time I set foot in the warehouse.'

Denise laughed. 'The only risk would be asking one of them out, and chancing chlamydia.'

The man at the bar had his wallet in his hand.

'See him?' Shelley and Denise swivelled to follow where Laurie was pointing. 'I'm going to ask him out.'

Shelley snorted. 'Twenty quid says you won't.'

The cocktail of fear, anger and excitement bubbling inside her exploded. She stood. 'Watch me.'

Before she could second-guess herself, she pushed her chair away and strode to the bar as the man hopped off his stool. She stood in front of him, so his back was to Shelley and Denise and they couldn't lip-read what she was saying.

'Hi, sorry to bother you. My name is Laurie. Could you possibly talk to me for ten minutes and pretend to enjoy the experience? Please?'

4

B en stared at the woman in front of him. His mind had been so full of work, it couldn't compute the abrupt shift from 'waste of an evening' to 'just died and gone to heaven'. Her hair hung in tight black curls around the softness of her face. Her eyes were almond-shaped, a shimmer of gold eyeshadow accentuating her glowing brown skin. And, *fuck me*. She was wearing glasses. His kryptonite. He blinked. How had he not noticed her before? Sure, for years there hadn't been any room in his life for love, or even sex, but he wasn't blind.

Her eyes crinkled with worry and she bit into her plump lower lip before speaking in a rush. 'I'm sorry, I'll leave you—'

'No!' He reached and caught her hand, interlacing his fingers with hers. 'I'm Ben.' She sucked in a breath and he saw her pupils dilate. Heat rushed to his cock. He tightened his grip.

She swallowed. 'Hi, Ben.' Her voice was a whisper.

'Why do you need to speak to me, and why do I need to pretend to like the experience?'

She looked down. 'I'm here with my work colleagues, and they... Don't look!'

He'd turned to see two older women sitting a few tables away, staring at him with stunned expressions. He winked at them, and their jaws dropped in perfect sync. He felt a tug on his hand and turned back to Laurie.

'Your work colleagues?'

'Shelley and Denise.'

'And they...?'

'Said I'm boring and never take risks, and bet me twenty quid I wouldn't ask you ou— talk to you.'

Ben's smile threatened to split his face in half.

'You want me to play along?'

'Only for a few minutes, if that's okay? I don't want to ruin your night.'

He stroked the back of her hand with his thumb. 'You've made my night.'

They stared at each other, both grinning like idiots. For the first time in as long as he could remember, work, and every other part of his life, vanished from his brain. He had achieved the kind of bliss state normally only obtained by meditating for decades in a cave.

'Why did you pick me?' he asked.

She blinked. 'Um, you were the only one available.'

The laugh burst out before he could stop it.

She looked horrified. 'I mean, it's Valentine's Day, so everyone's with someone, and... Oh god, do you have a girlfriend? Boyfriend?'

'I'm currently single.'

'Were you meant to be here on a date?'

'Business meeting. He stood me up.'

'I'm sorry.'

'I'm not.'

There was silence as the bubble they were in expanded. Ben felt like he already knew her on a soul level. The rest was just details.

'Tell me something about you that you'd never say out loud,' he asked. This was a game he'd picked up from his new loud American friend, Tabi when he was stranded in Chicago a couple of days ago. He saw her hesitate. 'No one else can hear. You can walk away at the end of tonight and never see me again.'

She took a big breath. 'Men don't want to be with me because I make them feel small.'

He tugged her closer. They were almost touching. 'How tall are you? You seem the perfect height to me.'

She licked her lips. 'I'm six foot.'

'Same here. So no sore neck from kissing you.'

He could see her breathing quicken. Her free hand rubbed the back of her neck, as if trying to calm herself.

'It's not only my height,' she stuttered. 'It's my brain. Most men don't like clever women.'

He raised his eyebrows. With every word she morphed more and more into the epitome of all his fantasies. So far, he'd kept his gaze trained exclusively on her face, but he longed to let it roam over her body.

'I find intelligent women a massive turn-on.'

She blinked again. 'You do?'

He nodded. 'And if they're wearing glasses, I'm a goner.'

She giggled. 'Do you have a librarian fetish, Ben?'

'I have a *sexy* librarian fetish. And I hope you noticed that I've yet to take my eyes off your face. I'm trying really hard to be a gentleman.'

She dipped her head and looked up at him through her long lashes.

'So, would your ideal librarian wear a pencil skirt?'

Ben closed his eyes and swallowed before he groaned audibly. 'Laurie, I swear to god, if you were dressed in a bin bag right now, all my fantasy librarians would start wearing them.'

She pulled his hand forward, splaying his fingers so his palm now rested against the curve of her hips. He opened his eyes and looked down.

'Laurie.' Her name sounded like a growl.

The sequins on her top sparkled, as if lighting the way to heaven. It was tight around her breasts, making him desperate to tear it off with his teeth, and her skirt ticked fantasy boxes he never knew he had. His unused libido quota from the past three years had just been unceremoniously dumped into his body. If his cock was hard before, now it was painful.

'Jesus, Laurie. You're so fucking hot I'm losing my mind.'

A gong sounded and she jumped, clutching at his arm and looking fearfully out into the room. He held tightly to her hip.

'Laurie, you okay?'

She shook her head and shivered. 'No. I'm petrified of animals.'

'Did you know where you were going tonight?'

She huffed. 'It was a surprise.'

'Do you want to leave? I can drive wherever you want to go.'

She looked at him, her eyes wide. 'I can't. I... '

The huge old doors at the end of the building opened with a loud creak and her head snapped around to face the sound. An elephant was lumbering into the room. Laurie stumbled back until she was standing against the edge of the bar. She looked terrified.

'Laurie, did you drive Denise and Shelley?'

She nodded.

'Let's get you out of here. You drive yourself home and I'll take your friends whenever they want to leave.'

'Are you sure?' Her voice was drowned out by the sound of the elephant trumpeting.

'Yes, of course. We'll get your bag, tell them what's going on, then get you out.'

She looked as if she was about to cry, but nodded, and pulled his hand to take him back to the table.

'Oy, oy!' said Denise. 'Our Laurie's actually pulled!'

'Have you given her a birthday kiss yet?' asked Shelley.

Ben looked at Laurie, who was taking cash out of her bag to put on the table. 'It's your birthday?'

Laurie grimaced at him and nodded. 'Shelley, Denise, I'm grateful for you taking me out tonight, but I've got to get out of here. I don't know how much it was but I'm leaving eighty quid just in case.'

'Woman!' a bird shrieked from near the door. 'Will you marry me?'

'But what about us?' complained Denise. 'We don't want to go. You can't abandon us, Laur. Chicks before dicks, love.'

Ben swallowed his irritation. These were her friends? 'You can leave now with Laurie or you can stay and I'll drive you home whenever you want to go.'

Denise elbowed Shelley. 'The dynamics of this throuple just changed, eh?'

Shelley raised her glass and winked at him. 'I hope you've got stamina, young man.'

He nodded at them and took Laurie's hand. He planned to walk her around the edge of the room to avoid most of the animals but had no idea how they were going to get safely past the elephant, still blocking the doors. He could hear a woman screaming 'yes!' over and over again, and the bird screeching 'Woman! Will you marry me?' as if someone had lost the off switch. They were half-way along the bar when a chimp leapt out and stood in front of them, teeth bared. *What the fuck?*

Where was its keeper? Ben assessed the room. The elephant was now blundering further inside, ignoring the tables filled with soon-to-be unhappy couples in its path. People were scrabbling to get out the way, and Ben could see the doors were now clear. He just needed to get Laurie past the chimp. It may have been small, but he knew it could rip his arm off without breaking a sweat. Out of the corner of his eye he saw a member of staff approaching with a bag of treats held out in front of him.

'Clarence! This way, buddy.'

Clarence scratched his backside and glanced between them and the man. He seemed to make a decision and held out both hands towards the bag.

'Lock the doors!' A man ran into the building, wearing combat fatigues and carrying a rifle. 'Lock the doors!'

The room went silent.

'The hippos! The hippos are loose!'

5

B en watched in slow-motion horror as the big wooden doors slammed closed and the elephant trumpeted. It sounded like a war cry, and the rest of the animals responded. Birds filled the air, shrieking and shitting. The elephant ploughed through the tables, and piglets squealed as they ran about hoovering up food from the floor. Clarence tore the bag of treats from his keeper, tipped the entire contents into his mouth, then dropped the packet and stared at them. His keeper turned and ran. *Oh fuck.*

'Laurie, climb over the bar and hide.'

'But, but what about y—'

'Laurie! Do it! Now!'

A switch had been flicked inside him. Gone was the workaholic businessman. Now Tarzan's more civilised younger brother was ripping his way out of an expensive suit and preparing to do battle to protect his woman. He'd never felt so brave. Laurie had awoken something inside him he never knew he had, and he never wanted to let it go. The instant connection he'd experienced with her felt like a lifeline to truly living.

Out of the corner of his eye he saw her disappear over the bar. Clarence moved, but Ben was quicker, grabbing a bar stool and holding it in front of him. The chimp hesitated, then jumped onto an empty table behind him, grabbed a bottle of wine and threw it. Ben fielded it with the chair and it smashed, showering him in glass and Pinot Noir. Clarence jumped up and down on the table, shrieking, then lobbed another at him. Suddenly a bottle flew past Ben's head coming the other way. He turned to see Laurie, her arms filled with alcopops. She was throwing them at Clarence, who sprang to another table to escape and grab more ammunition.

'Woman! Will you marry me?' A black bird swept low towards him. He dropped the bar stool to protect his head, and heard a cry from Laurie. He turned to see the bird flapping on her face. He lunged over the bar towards it as it took off.

'My glasses!'

Ben cupped Laurie's face. 'Are you okay?'

She was shaking and gasping for air but managed to nod. 'Ben, I can't see anything. Can you get us out of here? Do you know if Shelley and Denise are okay?'

Something crashed into his shoulder, and he turned, pushing Laurie behind him. Clarence was standing on the bar above them both, a bottle raised over his head.

'Laurie. On the count of three, I need you to run. One, tw — Aaaggghhh!'

Apparently Clarence hadn't learned to count and launched himself at Ben. All Ben saw were giant hairy hands, yellow teeth and a bottle of Scotch, before he fell to the floor, the wind knocked out of him. Was this how he was going to die? Being torn apart by a crazed chimp? Suddenly the hairy weight was lifted off him and he saw the face of the monkey's keeper, holding a dart gun.

'You okay, mate?'

Ben nodded, though he was screaming inside.

'Find your girl and take her through the door at the end of the bar. There's a staff room upstairs. Hunker down until the cavalry arrive.'

Ben got a hand up and ran down the back of the bar to where Laurie was standing, clutching a bottle for dear life.

'Laurie, come with me.' He pulled her through the door and they ran up a narrow flight of stairs. At the top, he checked the staff room was empty, then brought her inside and sat her down on a sofa. 'We're in the staff room. I'm going to call the police, then I'll go back and find your glasses.'

'Ben! You can't—'

'Which emergency service? All of them please. I'm calling from Buttley Manor... Uh, uh, okay, bye.' He finished the call, then dragged a large vending machine towards the door. 'They've already been notified. An armed response unit is on the way. I need you to push this against the door when I've gone, and don't open it unless whoever is on the other side is human-shaped and can say more than "woman, will you marry me?" Okay?'

Laurie sprang up and held onto his arms. 'Please don't go. It's only a pair of glasses.'

Ben had never felt so alive. The adrenaline had kicked his testosterone production through the roof, and now Laurie was safe, he was going to unleash his inner Rambo. He brushed his lips over hers and she whimpered.

'It's not only your glasses. It's your bag as well. And I'll see if I can find Shelley and Denise.'

Laurie nodded and pressed her lips to his, sweeping her tongue into his mouth. Desire raged through him like wildfire. He held her tightly, meeting her need with his own. Kissing Laurie felt like the ultimate prize for winning the game of life. Every decision, every sacrifice, had led to this bliss.

She broke the kiss, her breathing ragged. 'Forget my stuff. Find Shelley and Denise, okay?'

❦

LAURIE HEAVED THE VENDING MACHINE AGAINST THE DOOR as soon as Ben had left. She didn't know if her heart was pounding from physical exertion, stress, or the fact she'd never been so horny before. Ben was not only the best-looking man she'd ever met, but they were connected in a way that made her trust him implicitly. It was crazy, the strangest sensation, as if she knew Ben as well as she knew herself. To distract herself, she decided to inventory the vending machine. Everything was a blur without her glasses, but she knew it was from Somerset Snax, and also where each product would be. She peered through the glass, noticing they were completely out of cans of Blackcurrant Bliss. She would have to make sure they restocked on Monday and chase the extra order to make up for the pallet that was destroyed.

She stopped her train of thought, walked back to the sofa and sat. What was she thinking? She'd just turned thirty, survived an encounter with a maniac monkey and met a man who'd turned her world upside down. Was she really going back to work on Monday the same person? Could she carry on taking everyone's shit the same as she'd always done? Only a few hours ago she'd cut her supposed birthday cake and asked for more out of life. So far, this evening had fulfilled that wish in spades.

Adrenaline still rushed through her body and she shook out her hands, as if trying to discharge static electricity. Even though her sight was blurry, every other sense seemed heightened. Her skin tingled and every thud of her heart reminded her she was truly alive. She felt the most overwhelming urge to have sex with Ben. Raw, primal, unprotected sex. Now she'd nearly died, her body wanted to make up for this blunder by procreating.

She heard footsteps on the stairs and a knocking outside. 'Laurie, it's me, it's Ben.'

She pulled the vending machine to one side. He slipped through the gap, then barricaded the door again and put a pair of glasses in her hand. 'It's fucking carnage down there, but Shelley and Denise are fine. They're in the walk-in fridge. I've got your bag as well, so we just need to sit tight—'

'Ben!' With her glasses back on, Laurie could see it hadn't exactly been a teddy bear's picnic recovering her property. His pale skin was smeared with blood from deep scratches. His suit jacket was ripped; his knuckles were bleeding. She pushed off his jacket and ran her hands over his torn dress shirt. She tried to assess him for injuries, but all her traitorous mind seemed concerned with was the feel of his body. 'Are you okay?' she whispered.

He brought her hand to his lips and kissed it. 'Never felt better.'

She met his gaze and stared into his eyes, seeing a storm of want and need. The silence hung heavy between them.

She swallowed. 'Ben.'

'Yes, Laurie.'

She took a big breath. 'After a near-death experience, I think we need to reaffirm our commitment to life by having sex.'

6

Their lips crashed together and Laurie surrendered to the sensation of Ben's arms around her, his hot mouth drawing her into a boiling sea of pleasure. Every lick of his tongue, each press and caress, replaced her rational thoughts with an elemental language that translated as 'yes, more, NOW'. Whenever he broke the connection for a ragged breath, he stared at her with hooded, unfocused eyes and growled her name with an intensity that made her thighs quiver.

She yanked her skirt up and pulled his hand to her legs. She felt the heat of his touch as he dragged his fingers up her sensitive skin.

'Fuck, Laurie. Oh god, you're... I... fuck!'

If he sounded on the knife edge between pleasure and pain, then Laurie was already writhing in an agony of sexual frustration. She'd reached the point of no return, and if she didn't climax in the next five minutes, she was going to spontaneously combust.

'Ben, I need—'

He didn't hesitate, diving his tongue into her mouth and his hand inside her underwear. Her clit was throbbing, and when his fingers brushed against it, everything burst into flames. He didn't toy with her, he didn't explore, he simply found what made her moan, then did it again, and again, and again. She locked her arms around his neck, her forehead resting on his shoulder. She could no longer form words. Coherence had disappeared into cries. Hot rushes of pleasure roared through her as the glorious inevitability of her orgasm hurtled towards her.

'Yes, Laurie. Fuck, yes, yes.'

His voice pushed her over the edge and she stiffened with a silent scream. Her climax was an event horizon of light, eviscerating every cell, before sending her crashing and convulsing into another universe. Ben held her tightly as the pleasure continued to break her apart in waves. She drew in shuddering breaths. Had she actually combusted, or met god? The only thing she knew for sure was that this experience was utterly new, and now she wanted more. She lifted her head and their eyes met. He looked as stunned as she felt.

'Laurie, that was... ' He blinked and shook his head as if that might juggle his thoughts into order.

'Out of this universe.'

He nodded. 'I can't believe you're real. You're a goddess.'

Laurie felt her cheeks flush. His fingers were still gently stroking her. It was so intimate, but she didn't feel shy, she just felt her body revving up again. She reached between them and ran her hands over the outside of his trousers, feeling his hardness. He sucked in a breath and swore as she tugged down the zip and freed his cock. It was full and hot, the skin silky soft over a core of steel. She ran her thumb through the wetness seeping out of the slit, then wrapped her fingers around him and tugged. He let out a strangled cry and sank his middle finger deep inside her. She gasped and pumped him harder. He jerked back.

'Laurie, if you don't stop, I'm going to come.'

She put her hands on his chest, pushing him backwards until his legs hit the sofa.

'Sit.'

He sat with a thump. She grabbed her bag, unzipped an inner pocket and pulled out a crumpled condom packet. She peered at the back.

'Please tell me it's not expired,' he asked, hoarsely.

She smiled at him, then ripped it open with her teeth. 'We've got a month.'

His head fell back. 'I'm not going to last a minute.'

Happiness sparkled up inside her and burst out in a smile. She unfurled the condom over his length, biting her lip to contain a giggle as he groaned. She straddled him, pulled her panties to one side, and sank down with a sigh. He was so deliciously thick inside her and she yearned for more. She lifted up, then dropped back down.

'Ohfuckohfuckohfuckohfuck, Laurie!'

She laughed with joy and continued to move. She'd never felt so confident, so beautiful, so desired. Ben was staring at her with wild intensity, his hands gripping her hips, his neck corded with tension. She undid a button on her top, exposing more of her cleavage and his eyes bugged out. She lifted her hips up, paused, then dropped down as she popped another button.

'Laurie.' His voice was tight, as if he was teetering on the cliff edge of losing it.

She wanted to push him off.

Before she could second guess herself, she undid the final buttons, unclipped the front fastening of her bra and let her large breasts spill free.

The noise Ben made sent a thrill through her. It was the cry of a man being sexed to death. He fell on her breasts, sucking and pinching her nipples.

'Ben! Oh god, yes!'

As before, there was no subtlety, no slow build-up. He discovered what made her body sing, then cranked the volume up to eleven. She held his head to her chest as she moved faster, feeling the coiling pleasure building again. A zing ran through her clit as his fingers circled it. Her heart was pounding, increasing the pressure until every cell was primed to explode. Her climax detonated with sudden ferocity, her muscles clamping around his cock, as he pumped harder inside her. He followed her over with a yell, a guttural cry of victory, submission, and ultimate release.

Time seemed suspended as they made their way slowly back to earth. Laurie felt simultaneously languid and energised, and wholly alive. She peppered kisses across his forehead, then down his cheeks to his mouth. He wrapped his arms around her, as if he never wanted to let go, then drew his head back and looked at her.

'Woman. Will you marry me?' he squawked.

Laurie let out a peal of laughter that didn't stop. She was utterly, completely and deliriously happy.

'Although I'm going to have to take your last name,' he added.

She managed to control her giggles and raised an eyebrow. 'Why? What's your surname?'

'Driver. If you took mine, you'd be Laurie Driver.'

She snorted, then mentally paired his name with her surname and howled with laughter.

'What is it? What's your surname? It can't be worse than that?'

'It's Dover,' she guffawed. 'You'd be Ben Dover.'

His head jerked back. 'Woah. That's a lot to take in.' Then he wiggled his eyebrows and smiled. 'I'll do it. It's like losing a pound and winning Euro Millions.'

She kissed him, feeling suddenly shy. 'You're amazing.'

'You're the amazing one. Tell me, how did a Liverpudlian goddess end up in Somerset?'

'I went to Butlins on holiday when I was twenty and fell for someone from here. He got me a job at the company where he worked, and when we split up, he left and I stayed. I love the countryside around here, and if I ran back to Liverpool it would be as if I'd failed. I also have a really soft spot for the owner of the company.'

'A soft spot?'

'He's in his eighties. He's my West Country grandfather. Although he's hardly around anymore.'

'So you run it for him?'

Laurie let out a snort. 'In actuality, yes, in job title, no. I'm just an admin assistant who does everything from accounts to driving the forklift.'

Ben frowned. 'So what do the other staff members do?'

Laurie let out a puff of air. 'Make a five-minute job last all day, piss about on social media or wait for their turn to ask me to do their job for them.'

Ben looked confused. 'And you stayed? Why didn't you leave? Do something else?'

'If I left the company would collapse. I can't do that to my West Country grandfather. I did go for a promotion a while back, but he gave the job to someone who had been there longer than me. It's just how it is.' She sighed. Reality was seeping into the moment like a bad smell. 'So, future Mr Dover,' she said with a broad West Country accent. 'Where you be to then?'

Ben's face creased with a grin. 'You've got the lingo down

pat. Have you ever used that line on your family?'

'I once asked 'where that be to?' in reference to a bottle of ketchup, and my dad asked if everyone spoke funny down here.'

Ben nodded solemnly. 'He'd be right.'

Laurie giggled, aware she'd laughed more in one night than she had in years. 'But you don't have a West Country accent. I can hear an American twang in there.'

He stroked his finger down her cheek. 'Laurie Dover, you're incredible. You're the first person who's ever noticed. I did an MBA in the States and got a job there. I wanted to come back to be closer to my parents. I've only been back a couple of days.'

She heard a thundering of footsteps, then a loud banging on the door.

'Anyone in there?'

Laurie jumped up in panic, pulling the hem of her skirt down. Ben strode to the door, tucking himself back into his trousers and zipping them up.

'Yes, is everything under control downstairs?'

'It's contained. We need to take statements from everyone. Can you open the door?'

'Give me a moment.'

Laurie was struggling to refasten her bra and top. She stared at him in panic.

'You stay here,' Ben said. 'Let me see what they want and I'll come back for you as soon as I can. Okay?'

She nodded. Ben pulled the vending machine back enough so he could slip out the door. She heard their footsteps going down the stairs. Was it really okay down there? She shuddered. She only felt safe with Ben next to her; she didn't want to leave the room without him. Laurie straightened her clothes and sat on the sofa to wait. The sooner he came back, the better.

❧ 7 ☙

Ben didn't return. After ten minutes there were more footsteps, but it was two police officers. She pulled back the vending machine, and they entered the room and took her details.

'Can I leave now?' she asked. 'I need to find my friends.'

They shook their heads. 'This is an active crime scene. We need to take witness statements first.' The officer looked around her. 'We'll turn this into an incident room and start with you.'

'What are your friends' names?' asked the other officer.

'Shelley Lawler and Denise Taylor.'

He nodded. 'I'll go and let them know you're safe.'

IT FELT LIKE AN AGE BEFORE SHE'D GIVEN HER STATEMENT, and with every tick of the clock on the wall, she felt Ben slipping away from her. Where had he gone? Why hadn't he come back? She wasn't even allowed to leave the room on her own, as Harriet, one of the more aggressive hippos, was still on the loose. Finally, a man wearing a flak jacket, beard and grim expression escorted her down the stairs, an assault rifle wedged into his side.

The dining room was unrecognisable. Tables and chairs were scattered, and the floor was a mess of food, blood and shit. Laurie started shaking and the man put his hand on her arm.

'It looks worse than it is. No one's dead yet. Let's get you to your car.'

'Laurie!'

She turned to see Denise and Shelley teetering towards her. They looked surprisingly fine, except that the top of Shelley's dress had been lowered to the edge of her areola. Shelley took the officer's hand from Laurie's arm and clutched it to her chest.

'Thank you for bringing our baby back to us. You're our hero. Is there any way we can thank you, Mr...?'

The man tugged his hand back. 'I'll escort you to your car. Stay close.'

Denise pushed Laurie out of the way to get nearer the man with all the guns, but he stepped forward. 'I need you behind me.'

He led them back to the car park and they got into Laurie's car. She started it up.

'Thank you, Mr Bond,' said Shelley. 'You've saved our lives.'

The man bent down to Laurie. 'There's a checkpoint at the front gate. You need to stop there, okay?'

She nodded.

He pulled out a radio. 'Silver Ford Fusion leaving now with three females. Stand by for names and index number.'

Laurie pulled out onto the long drive and Shelley and Denise collapsed into shrieks of laughter.

'Oh my god, Shell, did you cop a load of him?'

'Bloody hell, yes. He just reversed the menopause!'

Laurie gripped the steering wheel tighter and gritted her teeth. Once Shelley and Denise had discussed every way they would have shagged Mr Armed Response, their attention turned to her.

'Where the hell did you disappear off to? You abandoned us,' accused Shelley.

'Yeah,' grumbled Denise. 'We were worried sick.'

'Ben said you were safe in the walk-in fridge.'

There was a pause long enough for Denise and Shelley to do some mental maths.

'Ooooh! You were with *Ben*, were you?'

'Were you giving him a lecture on health and safety?'

The banks of tolerance alongside River Laurie burst.

'Shut up! Shut up, the pair of you. I was terrified. And yes, I was with Ben. I was shagging him. I didn't have a birthday kiss, I had a birthday bang, and it was fucking awesome. Now don't say another word, or so help me god, I'm going to stop the car right now and you can both walk home.'

They were silent the rest of the journey.

❦

BEN: Sabrina, how's the date going? I've just met and lost the love of my life in a Jumanji near-death experience. Having a bit of trouble sleeping.

TABI: Yeah, yeah, Ben. Stop trying to steal Bree's thunder. Just because the hottest thing in your life is an Excel spreadsheet.

TRISTAN: Did you cop off with your business meeting? Robert someone-or-other? Fair play, mate.

TABI: And did you forget your safe word?

BEN: No! Her name is Laurie and she's everything I ever dreamed a woman could be.

TABI: And she tried to kill you with what, an elephant?

BEN: NO! Although if I don't find her again my life doesn't feel worth much anymore.

TABI: This seems a tad melodramatic, Ben. She ditched you after a couple of hours. But yeah, you should hunt her down. Ladies love a stalker.

BEN: No. We were separated after the police and special forces arrived to subdue the animals.

RORY: Now I'm listening.

JONATHAN: You're in Somerset, right? How scary are the sheep?

TRISTAN: Jonathan, pay attention. You're so obsessed with centrepieces and favours you failed to notice he's been at a safari park.

JONATHAN: For dinner? Oh, my expletive on a cracker. Eating exotic animals?

TABI: Yes, he had a hyena on a spit. Stick to picking cakes for your wedding.

TRISTAN: Ben, what happened?

BEN: I was leaving when this goddess asked me out. It was total love at first sight: rainbows, fireworks, unicorns.

JONATHAN: There are unicorns in Somerset? Did you eat the unicorns?

TABI: SHUT THE FUCK UP, JONATHAN!!!

RORY: Agreed. Now, can we skip to the part in the story with the special forces?

BEN: The animals went mental and started attacking everything and everyone. Then the hippos escaped.

RORY: Jesus. Hippos are fucking psychos. How many dead?

BEN: Not sure. It'll be on the news in the morning I expect.

TABI: Is this Laurie okay? Ben, sorry I was being an ass. I do that. Are you ok?

RORY: So mortal danger is the thing to turn you sincere? Good to know.

BEN: I'm ok. I left Laurie in a room behind a barricaded door.

JONATHAN: Do you have her number?

BEN: No, but I have her name and she lives in Somerset. I'll find her. I must.

TABI: Then it's settled. Now you HAVE to marry her.

JONATHAN: Yeah! Another wedding!

BEN: I know. She's the one for me.

TABI: Can't wait to meet Laurie Driver.

BEN: I'm taking her surname.

TABI: Really? Why? What is it?

BEN: Dover.

TRISTAN: Brilliant. Also, where's Sabrina? Can we track her on her mystery date?

RORY: On it.

WHEN LAURIE WOKE THE NEXT DAY, SHE LAY IN BED AND stared at the ceiling. She was sore in places she'd forgotten existed. That brought a smile to her face, but it soon fell off and disappeared into the aching hole in her chest. *Ben.* It all seemed like a dream. An experience too perfect to be true. Had he abandoned her? Or was he escorted out as they had been? She sighed and got out of bed. It didn't matter anymore. She would never see him again.

As she cleaned her flat, she decided her thirties would be different. From Monday, she was going to put some proper boundaries in place, starting with arriving at her contracted time of nine, rather than opening up the building at seven thirty. Her colleagues were going to get a big shock when she no longer picked up their slack. And if she couldn't get a promotion at Somerset Snax, she'd finally leave.

WHEN SHE STROLLED INTO THE OFFICE AT EIGHT FIFTY-NINE on Monday morning, Laurie's heart was thumping like a rebellious teenager attempting to get away with wearing make-up to school. Everyone was staring at her.

'You all right, Laurie?' asked Nathan with a frown.

She smiled. 'Great, thanks. How was your weekend?'

'Cool, cool, we had an engagement party on Saturday.'

'Lovely,' replied Laurie, sitting down at her desk and firing up her computer. She could hear Stacie hissing across the office at her fiancé.

'Er, it was a family thing, you know?'

Laurie pretended to be distracted with the contents of her bag.

'Anyway,' Nathan ploughed on. 'Where were you this morning? I got a call from Baz to say you hadn't opened up. Stace and I were, um, sleeping, and he woke us up.'

Pull up your big girl pants, drink a can of woman-up, grow a pair and rip this plaster off. Laurie took a big breath and turned to look at Nathan, a guileless smile on her face. She could feel everyone's eyes on her.

'I slept in, too. I didn't think there would be a problem as my hours are nine to five? I've also been thinking. I've been taking on too many tasks outside of my job description. I don't want you as the operations director to get into trouble. And I'm concerned about Mr Phillips falling foul of employment law or the HSE. So it's best for all concerned if I go back to the admin tasks I'm contracted to do.'

The room was silent, but the air crackled with energy, as fifteen people worked out how much time each day they would now have to divert from watching cat fail videos online.

'But, er, um,' stammered Nathan.

Whilst Laurie wanted to sit back and enjoy seeing Nathan's brain get pushed past tolerance, she also wanted to make it clear this conversation was over. So, she picked up a big pile of paper, leaned over her desk and put it on the one opposite her.

'Greg, I'm not going to be able to do these reports for you any more as I can't without an ACA qualification. It would be terrible if I made a mistake and you were blamed.'

Greg's mouth hung open and a half-eaten crisp fell out. The packet dropped out of his hand to the table.

Laurie picked up the phone on her desk and dialled. 'Good morning, this is Lauren Dover, the admin assistant at Somerset Snax. Our photocopier is playing up and I wondered if I could arrange for someone to come and take a look at it?'

The next hour was excruciating. Laurie finished her tasks for the entire week in a blur of activity, then panicked about how to fill the rest of her time. She was starting an inventory of every biro when the door opened and the owner walked in. She hadn't seen Mr Phillips in months. Each time he appeared, he looked frailer; but this morning there was a different air about him. He looked lighter, happier. As if he'd decided to press pause on his shuffle to the grave, so he could try out ballroom dancing.

Nathan leapt to his feet. 'Bob! Great to see you. To what do we owe the honour of this visit? Would you like a cup of tea? Laurie! Tea for Mr Phillips. One milk, two sugars.'

Bob Phillips patted Nathan on the arm. 'Laurie knows it's white, no sugar, don't you, love?' He winked at her. She smiled and went to the kitchen.

When she returned, the room was filled with the entire staff of Somerset Snax. She handed Bob his tea, then went to stand at the back.

'So,' he began. 'I've been spending some time talking it over with Sue, and we've decided it's time. I'm selling the business.'

A shocked gasp rippled around the room and Bob put his hands up.

'This is all for the better. The new owner is young and excited about taking this company to the next level. I think all of us know this has been long overdue.'

'Er, when is this happening?' stuttered Nathan, clearly out of the loop.

Bob clapped his hands together. 'Today! He's due any minute. I want to introduce him to everyone.'

On cue, the doorbell rang.

'Wait there!' Bob exclaimed, like a magician about to pull the rabbit out of the hat. He walked out the door, and the room broke into a frenzied murmur of conversation Laurie wasn't part of. She was glad for Bob. It was the right decision for him and the company. Hopefully the new owner would get everything back on track.

Bob opened the door and everyone surged forward. For once, she couldn't see past them.

'So, ladies and gents,' she heard Bob announce. 'Let me introduce you to your new boss, Mr Ben Driver.'

8

Laurie stumbled backwards against a window, the metal Venetian blinds clattering noisily. Ben? Here? Her *boss*?

'Hi, everyone, I'm Ben and I'm excited to get to know you all.' His voice carried across the room.

Laurie hung her head. It *was* him. Even if she'd wanted to stay at Somerset Snax, now she couldn't. She'd shagged her boss and bragged about it to the biggest gossips in the building. And she'd also told him she ran the show as the rest of his staff were utterly incompetent. Oh fuck. Oh fuckity, fuckity, fuck. Her thirties had begun with a bang, but were now a smoking ruin.

'Hi, Ben, I'm Shelley, nice to meet you.'

Laurie heard Denise snort. Even though she was slouching against a radiator, there was no escape. The crowd was breaking up as he made his way through the room, shaking everyones' hands. She had seconds before he saw her.

'And this is Laurie,' said Bob. 'Our admin assistant and maid of all work.'

Laurie straightened as her eyes met Ben's. His smile was so big, her heart skipped a beat.

'Hi, Laurie.' He took her hand and a thrill ran up her arm. Ben turned to Bob, a quizzical look on his face. 'Maid of all work?'

Bob chuckled and held up his mug. 'Laurie's our secret weapon. If you want your tea done right, go to her. And she can drive a forklift.'

Ben stared blankly at him. Laurie suddenly saw Bob Phillips in a whole new light, and it wasn't particularly flattering. 'I'd like to start today by speaking privately to everyone here,' said Ben. 'Find out more about them and what they do.' He turned to her. 'Laurie, I'd like to start with you, if that's all right?'

'Oh, no, son, you need to start at the top,' replied Bob, steering him away. 'Nathan! Come and have a chat with Mr Driver in my... Ha! I mean *his* office. You know, Ben, Somerset Snax would fall apart if it wasn't for our Nathan.'

NATHAN WAS IN BEN'S OFFICE FOR OVER AN HOUR. BEN HAD asked him to bring his laptop in, and when he finally emerged, red-faced, he stalked over to Stacie's desk and whispered furiously at her. The whole office was silent, but as soon as everyone heard the words 'search history', 'cats', and 'porn hub', the clattering of fingers on keys made the room sound like a typewriting pool from the nineteen fifties. Only Laurie noticed Ben opening his office door and watching them, his arms crossed and a grim expression on his face. He cleared his throat and everyone jumped and looked up.

'I thought I'd let you all know that before I completed my MBA, I did a double major in computer programming and accountancy, specialising in forensic work.' He lifted a piece of paper. 'Greg Parfitt? Can we have a chat now?' Greg looked behind him, as if hoping another Greg Parfitt would suddenly materialise to take the fall, or if he could get to the doors and escape without being noticed. His shoulders eventually sagged in defeat, and he dragged himself out of his chair like a reticent member of the newly undead and shuffled towards Ben.

As soon as the door closed, Shelley and Denise were out of their chairs like a pair of electrocuted harpies. They perched on Laurie's desk, flanking her.

'What the fuck did you say to him?' hissed Shelley.

'Why is this anything to do with me?' she whispered back.

Denise gave a loud harumph. 'Well you obviously did more than just shag—'

'Shut up! Keep your voices down.' Laurie was beside herself. She didn't know whether to burst into tears, throw up, or scream. Thankfully fury won the emotion war. 'The professional competency of each person in this business has nothing to do with me, and is not my responsibility. Do you honestly think any new owner wouldn't do whatever he's doing?'

Shelley and Denise opened their mouths to speak, but Laurie cut them off.

'No. Don't you dare say a word to anyone.'

Denise leaned forward. 'And what's our silence worth eh, Laurie?'

Laurie swallowed the bitter taste in her mouth. Her job was over, but she wanted to leave with her reputation and dignity intact. 'I'll see what I can do.'

Denise and Shelley nodded slowly, like middle-aged Mafioso bosses, then walked back to their desks.

'Is everything all right over there?' Stacie called across the room.

'Yeah fine. ' Denise smiled. 'Everything's peachy.'

❦

TWO HOURS LATER, BEN WAS ABOUT TO BLOW A FUSE. HE'D worked his way through the bright lights of Somerset Snax and discovered they were actually forty-watt bulbs with the filaments about to snap. He shut the door behind another work-shy underperformer and raked his hands through his hair. What the actual fuck had he done? He'd worked without a break for years. Saving every penny, every cent. Denying himself a life for the dream of owning his own business back home. And in his excitement, he'd trusted how it looked on paper and the say-so of a man who'd placed Laurie at the bottom of the pecking order.

Laurie.

Ben smiled as his heart leapt and his body burned. On Friday night he'd been forcibly ejected from Buttley Manor by a man who outmatched him by six inches, an assault rifle and a handgun. He'd been desperate to get back to Laurie but knew he would find her again. He had her full name and more determination than Prince Charming seeking Cinderella. He just didn't expect to see her first thing Monday morning at his new company.

He relived the panic on her face and the smug smiles of Denise and Shelley. She may have been worried, but he didn't give a flying fuck he was her boss. She was the most incredible woman he'd ever met, and he never wanted to let her go. As crazy as it felt, he'd happily sell Somerset Snax tomorrow if it would put her mind at rest. And he was glad she'd told him about the state of the company. It meant he could find out in a day what would have taken weeks to uncover. Looking back over the figures, sales reports, and through people's laptops, it was clear where Laurie had been. There would either be patches of perfect work, or a moment where it was obvious she'd completely taken over. Was Bob Phillips so far removed he'd failed to notice? Or was he simply a misogynistic twat? To Ben, Laurie's brain was the ultimate turn-on. The fact that it lived in the body of a goddess was just the cherry on top of the icing on the cake. He just had to chew through the rest of the staff, then he could get to her. He smoothed down his hair and opened the door.

'Shelley Lawler, do you want to come on through?'

Shelley didn't move. She looked like a poker player who held all the cards and didn't care who knew it.

'I'm just about to go on my break,' she replied casually, leaning further back in her chair. 'Why don't you see Laurie next?'

He let Shelley's attitude slide and turned to Laurie, his heart lightening. 'Laurie Dover?'

She nodded, stood and strode past him into his office. He shut the door behind her. *Finally.*

'Laurie—'

'I'm resigning. With immediate effect. I've got four weeks of holiday to take. That will cover my notice period.'

'What? Why?'

Her hands were balled into fists by her sides. 'Why do you think?'

'Is this because I didn't come back? Fuck, I tried, but a scary bastard tooled up like the Terminator frogmarched me to my car. I—'

'No. I'm leaving because I had sex with my boss, told him confidential information about his company, and betrayed the trust of my colleagues. So I can either perform some kind of Jedi mind trick to make you forget everything I said, persuade you Shelley and Denise are the hardest workers here and deserve a pay rise, or walk out the door and never come back.'

'You can't do that. You can't leave.'

'I don't have a choice. Everyone's already pissy with me because I told them this morning I wasn't going to do their jobs any more. Now you're finding the skeletons in their closets and they want someone to blame. There's no way Shelley and Denise will be able to keep their mouths shut. My life here was just about tolerable, but now it's going to be hell. I can't live like that.'

'You can't be the one to lose out here. Fuck, I'll sell the company tomorrow if you'll stay.'

She shook her head, frowning. 'That's crazy. You can't do that, and it won't stop people from finding out I slept with my boss and dobbed them all in it.'

'You didn't sleep with your boss, you slept with me. That was Friday and this is Monday. And you didn't do anything to anyone. You gave me no details and no names. The only thing you did was help me discover sooner rather than later they've been taking the piss.'

'Ben, you don't get it. Nothing about this is going to work.'

He froze. 'What do you mean? What about us?'

She raised her hands, as if trying to show him the truth he was trying to avoid.

'There is no us! After this there can never be an us!'

He ran his hands through his hair in frustration. 'Laurie. Meeting you was the most significant thing that has ever happened to me.' He gestured around him. 'Bigger than this, bigger than anything.' He reached for her and she crossed her arms over her body. 'I meant every word I said on Friday night.' He held her gaze, willing her to remember. 'Even when I was pretending to be a bird.' Her lips parted with a silent 'oh', then clamped shut again. 'Please, Laurie. Give us a chance. I'll always have your back. We'll get through this together.'

'No. We can't and we won't.' Her bottom lip was wobbling. 'I've got to go.'

'Laurie—'

'Don't. Please, Ben.'

She walked out the door and closed it behind her. He stood in silence, watching her through the window. She put a coffee mug bearing her name in her bag, deposited a set of keys on the desk, grabbed her coat and walked out. She was gone.

9

BEN: *Urgent. Anyone there? Need help.*

    SABRINA: OMG did you find Laurie?

    BEN: Yes. But not good.

JONATHAN: Elaborate. How can we get this true love back on track?

BEN: ...

SABRINA: Tris, Rory, you online?

BEN: ...

SABRINA: Come on, guys, I know you've seen these messages.

BEN: ...

SABRINA: Ugh! WAKE UP, TABI! I don't care if it's four in the morning in Sonoma. I need support here, not two emotionless British dudes and the Hallmark quoting farm boy fiancé.

TRISTAN: We can't offer support until we know what the problem is. And we have emotions. We just don't go waving them around willy-nilly like Americans.

BEN: ...

SABRINA: Willy-nilly? OMG, TABI, WHERE ARE YOU? I need estrogen and sarcasm back up.

BEN: I've discovered Laurie, who is apparently the only woman I will ever truly love, works for the company I just bloody bought. They've all been doing fuck all for years while she does everything. Two of her colleagues know we shagged and it's gone tits-up. She resigned and left. Now, everyone will think I'm firing people because of her and not their browser histories.

SABRINA: Um. That's super crazy. Love?

TRISTAN: You shagged her? Fair play, mate. Fair play.

BEN: She's incredible. I've waited my entire life to find someone this strong, funny, gorgeous and who wears glasses. I don't give a fuck about the company any more, I just want her.

SABRINA: I feel ya. It's a zing thing.

TRISTAN: Where is she now? I will mock you later Sabrina for your 'zing thing'.

BEN: I presume she went home but I don't know where she lives.

TRISTAN: Look up her personnel file.

BEN: I can't do that, it's a breach of data protection.

RORY: Grow a pair.

TRISTAN: Drink a can of man-up.

SABRINA: Really Tris? 'Man- up?' Is that a real thing? If it is, then 'zing thing' is real.

JONATHAN: I agree with the Brit boys. Pull your socks up, or whatever it is you do over there.

RORY: Ben, if she means that much to you get off the fucking phone and get her back. I would have given up everything for Zoe. The title, the castle, the estate, everything. Just fucking go.

SABRINA: Hold up. What? Rory, dear, you have a castle? What the fuck? What kind of title? Tabi is going to be all over this! Ben, what are you gonna do? You have to figure it out.

SABRINA: Ben? You still here?

SABRINA: Ben??????

. . .

BEN PULLED UP LAURIE'S RECORDS, HIS FINGERS SHAKING with adrenaline. He put her address and mobile number in his phone, then exited his office, ignoring the stares. It was quicker to get to the car park through the warehouse so he went that way. Blood was roaring in his ears, every sense focused on getting to Laurie. His unconscious mind clocked the warehouse was busy and negotiated him around the pallets. In front of him, a forklift was stacked so high he couldn't see the driver. He stopped. *Is that safe? How can they see where they're going?*

The forklift started towards him. Ben called out but it didn't stop. Behind him and to the sides were walls of pallets, above him the metal shelving units. Fuck! He leapt on top of a pallet of drinks, waving his arms.

'Hey! Stop!'

Ben could just about make out the head of a young man, headphones wedged into his ears. His eyes were closed and he was singing. The pallet on the front of the forklift was getting closer and closer. 'STOP!' he screamed. The young man's eyes snapped open and he stared at Ben in shock, as if waking from a nightmare. 'BRAKE!' A look of vague comprehension seemed to cross his face and he nodded. *Thank fuck.*

The forklift sped up.

Ben was aware of a whole- body punch, then everything went black.

THERE WAS ALWAYS A LOT OF WEATHER ON THE MENDIPS, but the blurriness through the windscreen of Laurie's car wasn't caused by rain. She had allowed her tears to fall the moment she pulled out of Somerset Snax, and now they wouldn't stop. Less than a mile down the road, it became dangerous to drive and she pulled into a passing place by the entrance to a field and cut the engine.

The dam broke on everything she'd held in for the last eight years. All the loneliness and disappointment of her twenties flooded out. She finally allowed herself to acknowledge the wasted years, the regrets that she didn't push harder for recognition and respect, and the realisation it had all been for nothing. Layered on top of the pain of her past was the empty wasteland of her future. No job. No career. No relationship. She'd never met anyone like Ben. Someone who was turned on, not off, by her height and the size of her brain. It was like experiencing the light of heaven, then having it snuffed out before your eyes and knowing the rest of your life would always be dark and empty.

I meant every word I said on Friday night. Even when I was pretending to be a bird.

His words slipped like strands of sunlight into the depths of her grief.

Please, Laurie. Give us a chance. I'll always have your back.

She thought back to Friday night. He'd been willing to sacrifice himself for her. She was always the strong one, but he'd been her protector. He'd put her first without hesitation. Would Shelley or Denise, or any of her friends have done the same? Her tears stopped and she stared, unseeing out the front window. Of course they wouldn't have. Just like at work, they would use her to their own advantage when it suited them. And not only would she let them, she was now running away from her biggest chance at happiness. A flash of anger surged through her. Why should she give up Ben for them? Why didn't she deserve happiness? Sure, it was going to be hell at work, but why should she suffer for their sins? She started the car and turned around. Ben had fought for her and now it was her turn to fight for him.

Pulling into the car park, fear knifed through her at the sight of an ambulance outside the warehouse. Two paramedics were running inside and she followed them in. A forklift lay abandoned, under the shelving unit that had been damaged on Friday. Sandwiched between the boxes it had been carrying and the next pallet was a body. Ben. Despite her explicit instructions, and the obvious stupidity of the idea, the warehouse staff had continued to stack the unstable shelving, and now the pallet above the forklift was tipping. The ashen-faced staff stood like zombies, doing nothing to help as one paramedic rang the police and fire brigade and the other rummaged in his pack. Laurie didn't know if Ben was dead or alive, but she had to get him out of there. If she didn't, and the pallet fell, it would crush him. She climbed into the cab and started it up.

'Miss! Get out, it's not safe!' Arms pulled at her, but she shook them off. A loud creak sounded above her and cans started raining down on the cab.

'Laurie!' screamed Stacie.

She reversed the forklift back, then jumped out, ran underneath the shelving and climbed on top of the pallet. Ben was slumped on his side, immobile. She pulled him to the edge, leapt off, and heaved him over her shoulders. She staggered out, cans raining down. There was an almighty crash, and the entire pallet came thudding down, right where Ben had just been lying.

Laurie was aware of screaming, but it sounded very far away. A paramedic helped Ben off her shoulders and they laid him on the ground. Even though the paramedics were assessing him, she held his hand and her breath, praying to every god she knew. She felt a squeeze on her fingers and his eyes fluttered open.

'Laurie?'

'Sir, can you tell us your name and date of birth?'

Ben ignored them. 'Laurie. You came back.'

She nodded, tears falling. 'You were right. We'll get through this together.'

'How are you feeling? Can you move your feet for us?'

Ben turned to the paramedic. 'I'm fine. I've never felt better.'

'We're going to move you to hospital now. Miss, can you get back please?'

Ben held her hand tighter and pulled her towards him. His lips grazed her ear. 'Laurie, after a near-death experience, I think we need to reaffirm our commitment to life.'

A laugh bubbled out of her. 'By having sex?' she whispered.

She felt his cheek touch hers as he smiled. 'Yes, and other things.'

THE END

EPILOGUE

T ABI: *All of you listen to me. You idiots need to keep your crises and texts to PST. Got me? Pacific Standard Time. Now. What happened with Ben?*

RORY: Typical Yank, thinking the rest of the world doesn't exist when you're asleep. Have you even read the chat?

TABI: Keep a lid on it, bagpipes. And yes, I just have. Shit. Do we know if he found Laurie or why he hasn't answered us? I have friends in the UK that could see if he's ok. And we WILL get to the castle thing in a moment.

SABRINA: I see how you are, Tabi. You'd call out international search and rescue for Ben, but when I go missing on my blind date, you just figure, 'oh well, she's dead'.

TRISTAN: Bree, you're less fragile than Ben. Tab, we've heard nothing from him.

BEN: Hello, everyone, this is Laurie here, Ben's, um, well, girlfriend. There was an accident in the warehouse earlier and Ben was knocked unconscious. We're in hospital now and he's with the doctors, but he's going to be fine. He wanted me to message you all to thank you for your advice!

SABRINA: Yayayayayayayayay! He found you! Or you found him?

JONATHAN: I love all this love! Relieved he's good. Heading to a cake tasting. Tough work.

TABI: Thank God. And hi, Laurie. Girlfriend, huh? Nice work, sister. Now, Rory, back to that title and castle thing. I have WTAF questions.

RORY: Laurie, let us know if there's anything we can do. And bugger off, Tabi.

THE END. FOR NOW...

II

STUPID CUPID

by
Kelly Kay

PROLOGUE

February 12 – Chicago, IL
United Lounge, O'Hare airport
4:28 p.m. US CST

SABRINA

I pour another glass of this insanely good red wine that my new super-close friend, Tabi, makes. She actually makes it or owns the winery. I'm not clear. There's been drinking. We're stuck in the United Club lounge at O'Hare airport. My sisters are pissed that my plane isn't in New York. Like I'm the one who blew up the transformer. The more I sip the less I am caring about my annoying family. I am now pretty well super drunk in my head thinking of things.

The six of us were strangers. And now, by the magic of kick-ass Cabernet, we're not. These are my bestest friends. I'm so lucky to have these people who I've known for like four hours now. Tabi's laugh is as big and bold as she is. The giant gruff Scotsman is sitting next to me. He keeps moving my wine away from me and I give him a little side-eye.

"Sabrina, you're drinking head-to-head with some professionals. Mind yourself."

"You mind yourself," I say to him. Wow, he is crooked looking. No. Nevermind. That's me. I am sitting crooked. There. I sit up and Rory is not crooked.

He laughs a low grumble, and I smile. He's watching out for me. That's different. I like it. He smells of heather. I have no fucking clue what heather smells like, but I imagine he's made of peat, heather, and tartan. His dirty blonde hair is long, curly disheveled and he looks stern. He keeps rolling his eyes at Tabi, yet sticks around to hang out with us. He's a reluctant sweetheart of a giant man.

I yell, "Hey, Tristan, fancy snooty-pants!"

"Yes, small, clever blonde American."

"I think you're funnier than you're letting us know."

"Perhaps, but someone needs to maintain some decorum."

I think he looks as charming as Americans think Hugh Grant is. I fill his glass up and his fabulous smile erupts. This weekend was supposed to be chocolate and Netflix with my nieces, but my perfect sister is forcing me to go on a blind date for fucking Valentine's Day. "Trisssian. Teel us a secrets." Damn that wine.

Tris says, "Not so clever after some wine. Ok, I'm not who you think I am."

Tabi makes a fart noise with her mouth. "LAME. Super fucking lame. I really need pickles or capers. Like a salty, juicy thing. But for now, tell me something juicy."

Rory rolls his eyes and Jonathan and I crack up.

"You first." Jonathan is a wall of farmer muscle. I'm sure he's not drunk; he's enormous, it would probably take a straight week of drinking to get him buzzed. He's a white blond mountain.

Tabi sips, then says, "I was once the object of a senatorial sex scandal. Drink up, bitches!" She grins as if she's thrilled this happened to her.

Rory raises his water to her. "Not surprising."

Ben looks at her and says, "Holy shit. I've been living in the states. I know this—it's a rather dirty tale."

Tabi sloshes her wine around. "Everyone knows it."

I jump up. "Tabitha Aganos! Baxter Schroeder. Shit. I knew I knew you. THE FUCK IT LIST!" I say reverently.

"The list." She nods and shoves cheese in Jonathan's mouth. He laughs and swallows it whole.

She points to the other men. "Bax is my husband, so it's all cool, you judgy Brits. New game: for each tale someone tells, I'll send you a case of wine. And I'll send you a case of lemons, Rory sour-face." He smirks. "Or a case of chocolate of your choice." He raises an eyebrow and silently toasts her with his bottle of water.

"I'm moving home because I've bought a company I've never seen before. I'm totally going to fail. And I prefer red," Ben says.

Tristan says, "Atta boy." He raises his glass and drains the whole thing in like one sip, and I can't look away from his big lips. They're huge. I don't like huge lips. Maybe they're not. I squint my eyes to stare and see if they really huge lips and Tab interrupts my brain.

She points at me. "Hmm, Sabrina Faire, get to talking."

And somehow, having spent only four hours with these people, I'm closer to them than my actual friends. "I award scholarships to people at the Art Institute and I don't know the difference between Degas, Monet, or Manet. My sisters usually find me invisible. And I don't date because men either make me feel small or run. Or I try to change myself to date them." Wow, that little therapy piece slipped out. I slam my hand over my mouth.

Tabi leans towards me and says in the calmest voice she's used yet, "That's all bullshit, you know? Red, white, or mixed?"

I nod and grin. "Red, please."

Rory nudges me to eat some cheese. I shove some crackers in my mouth. I could use some brothers in my life. I smile at him, then look at the group. "And I have a blind date on Valentine's Day with a man named after a penis." Everyone starts laughing.

Tabi says, "You going for two cases?"

Jonathan blurts out, "I'm not sure I'm not still in love with the love of my life and if she was my everything."

Ben says, "Good thing you're getting married."

"She's not the one I'm talking about."

The five of us scream, "Oh!"

I blurt out, "Snap, that's rough."

Tabi leans over to Jonathan. "Do you want me to give you all the wine for your wedding?" He nods, smiling. "Then marry the right girl."

He's still nodding. "I will. That was drunk talk. She's long gone, and I love Tanya."

Rory says to me, "And you don't know the penis bloke at all?"

I shake my head.

Jonathan puts his hands out. "It will be love, Bree. My fiancée and I are so desperately in love we communicate telepathically."

Ben says while he sips, "So, you don't talk?"

He begins to justify and we all laugh at him. "We know each other's souls. We don't need all the details of life."

Tristan says, "So, you don't actually know her?"

Jonathan continues, "We don't have to paw at each other to prove our affection." He's getting red-faced, and it's hysterical to watch the Brits take him down.

We're all laughing, as Rory leans over and says, "So, you don't actually have sex?"

"She's saving herself for marriage. Well, she's saving herself from me for marriage."

Tabi says, "That's a fuck of a dry spell. How long?"

"Six months. I can wait for Juliet. Can I have more wine please?" Jonathan asks. We stare at him.

Tristan crosses his legs and leans towards Jon. "Thought her name was Tanya?" We all hoot again. His face gets red and flustered and he grabs the bottle and drains it.

Tabi puts her phone on the table. "Numbers. I'll text for shipping addresses. Jon, I'll send wine for whomever you marry. Ten cases good? Don't tell Bax I gave away wine. My partners hate it when I do that, but oh well."

Tristan picks up the phone, and Tabi glares at him. "Spill it snooty-britches." I spit up a little red.

"Fine, if I must, and only because you're strangers. I might be in love with a woman and I've never seen her legs. Or in three dimensions. I call it *my secret Zoom shame*. Mixed case, please."

There's a long silence while we sip. It's our first pause in conversation and I'm stunned Tabi hasn't filled the void. I move in the leather seat that's starting to stick to me. I try to get up but slide off the chair and land on the ground. We all laugh except Rory who is there with a hand to help me up. As I head to the ladies' room, Ben calls after me, "What's the dick's name? The one you have a date with?"

I turn and smile. "Ricky Schlong." Hysterical laughter follows me as I stumble down the hall.

. . .

I'M SO FUCKING WASTED I DON'T EVEN KNOW HOW I FOUND the plane. I turn my phone in my hand and there are two million texts waiting. My sisters are a panicky sort. They need to chill. I'll get to New York in time to meet the penis man.

TABI: 'Sup bitches. Miss me?

BEN: In a strange way, yes, I do. But I am grateful to be headed to my gate.

JONATHAN: You guys are like my bestest friends. Like, bestest. Love you.

TRISTAN: So bloody tired. Good night, all. Safe travels.

I type out carefully.

SABRINA: Thank you all for hanging out with me. I feel good. I mean I feel gooder than I did about my life.

JONATHAN: We're bonded FOR LIFE. SSSSSSSSabrina checks in when you s*/o on the date. I hate worry. fingers are fat and my phone is ttiny m

RORY: Tabi, I thought our mobile numbers were for our delivery addresses, not to burn through my international data?

TABI: This is more fun than shipping addresses. Happy flights.

RORY: Sabrina. I second Jonathan's drunken sentiment. Check in. Let us know you're safe. And, Tabi, and I mean this from the bottom of my kilt you like to pretend I'm wearing, fuck all the way off.

TABI: I'll miss you too, Rory.

10

February 14 – New York City

SABRINA

SABRINA: *This is the dumbest thing I've ever done.*

JONATHAN: *You gotta believe. Believe this is the man for you.*

SABRINA: *Who flies to another city for a blind date? My perfect sister is a moron with terrible taste. Why did I think she could choose a mate for me?*

TRISTAN: *I'm up as well. Was on a video chat with an American colleague. Bree, perhaps stop using the word 'mate'.*

SABRINA: *I don't trust romance and Valentine's Day. What if he tries to kill me? There's that. It could happen.*

JONATHAN: *Quit bitching. Go fall in love. Some of us love Valentine's Day. You're only in Manhattan for one more night. Enjoy it. If you'll excuse me, I have a fiancée to woo. Flowers, candy, music.*

TABI: *Good fucking night, that's schmaltzy. Tris, go to bed. Bree, get your rocks off and fuck the stranger. Fucking strangers is almost always a good idea. I miss fucking strangers.*

SABRINA: Really?

TABITHA: Nah. I fucking love fucking my husband. Never grows old. But having been with my fair share of strangers—long story —there's a magic in that too. It's just a date. Go. RORY! What do you think? Rory, I know you're looking. Come on, you cranky tartan wearing tart. Let's go, you grouchy Scotsman. Answer us. Give us a little kiss.

RORY: Why the fuck am I on this chat?

SABRINA: Sorry to bother you, Rory, but you're a part of this now.

RORY: Is there one of those emoji things for sighing? I'll be a silent observer, if Tabitha leaves me the fuck alone.

JONATHAN: You don't need luck, just heart—open it up. Did you wear the blue dress?

SABRINA: [picture of sapphire blue dress with sheer sparkly thigh highs and strappy high heels].

TRISTAN: Bloody hell, you look lush. Your hair looks like a blonde waterfall.

TABI: What does 'lush' mean? She's not a fucking rainforest.

SABRINA: I'd rather be in a rainforest. I'm comfortable with just me right now. Love has to wait.

RORY: Famous last words.

I smile as I put my phone away. I know these random people will fade with time, but we're bonded from being stuck at the airport for now. They're funny, and all my real friends are tired of hearing about my dating life, or lack of one. Chicago seems to be a revolving door of the same men over and over. I'm exhausted from trying not to date the same guy I met on Bumble a year ago. Or running into the same work colleague I mistakenly slept with two years ago at some after-work dive.

I sit at the bar and am surrounded by all the lovey-dovey

faces. I take faith that nothing ever works out for me. It's familiar, and I've become the master of the pivot in life. I gesture to the adorable bartender. It's a shame he's not my date. He's not wearing a red striped tie. And his name tag doesn't say Ricky. Ricky Schlong. My sister made a point of telling me it's pronounced Schlein. But it's still Schlong, and I hope he's not one. There's no silent g. Come on, it's Schlong. And she informed me he's shorter than me. I'm not tall. I tried to clarify, mailbox short or Tom Cruise short? She didn't answer.

In forty-seven minutes, I have an Uber coming. I've already planned my escape from the Schlong. My car will take me back to the romantic hotel my other sister booked. Her husband had points or something, and apparently my whole family is rooting for the Schlong because it's a suite at the Plaza. After a good night's sleep, I'll hop on my very early flight and be home to Chicago by lunch.

I smile at the insanely handsome, not Ricky, bartender. "Martini, please."

"Chocolate?"

"Hell, no. Because I'm a woman?" Maybe my back is a tiny bit up.

He smirks and pushes a placard to me. It's the drink special of the night.

"Sorry," I say. "I'm a bit keyed up. Gin, up, dry with a twist. Please."

"On it." He winks. And now he's ruined his own mystique. I'm not sleeping with a winker. And you know Schlong is a winker.

No one is looking around, just me. I'm the only one here for a blind date on Valentine's Day. A whoosh of cold air cyclones around me, and I glance towards the front door. Tight, neatly done tawny hair, golden-green hazel eyes, tall, broad shoulders, when he smiles at the host I hold my breath. It's a kind of cockeyed smile that says he's not going to take anything too seriously, but everything matters. Everyone around him lights up. He's wearing a deep charcoal cashmere coat, buttoned up, and black leather gloves. It's not bitter cold tonight, but it's still February in New York. I sit up straight, tug my deep V-neck into place, and flip my cascading hair behind me. Please, god, let his tie have red stripes. The hostess laughs, and he appears to fake laugh back at her. The air in the room eases around all of us. He's got that thing certain people have. I don't. But he does—the thing that sets everything right with his smile.

He's looking around, and my breath catches. Anticipation crashes over my skin, leaving a trail of goosebumps in its wake. Maybe my sister doesn't have shit taste in men. Perhaps she's a matchmaking genius, and this man, who does something vague and suspicious in the medical or construction field, is actually this sophisticated and stunning gentleman. The way he moves, so sure of himself, is enough to sell me on him. I want to climb him. And I'm super unmotivated to rock climb, mountaineer, or adventure anything at all. But this. This man is my Everest. I will summit him. I want to set up my tent at his base camp. I need the oxygen to thin and to hallucinate and see stars in front of my eyes. I'd actually exercise if I could have this man.

11

PATRICK

I t's like the lights dimmed in the rest of the restaurant, and there's a spotlight on her. I'm a little lightheaded, locking eyes with her in a way that suggests I've taken a blow to the head. It could be a stroke. I feel under my glove for my pulse. It seems fine.

I break our gaze for the briefest of seconds to let my eyes rake down her body. And fuck it all. Fuck it right up the middle. Fuck all the diners and bosses and assholes because she's wearing a blue dress that matches her electric eyes. Who has bright enough eyes to be seen all the way across the room? They're like beacons or a lighthouse calling my cock to shore. Why can't that one be mine? I scan the room for the yellow-dress woman I'm supposed to meet. Melanie Tinywhole. I'm told it's pronounced Tihinyho. Either way, it's fucking bad. She sent me a Google audio file that pronounced her name for me. I giggle every time I say it either way.

She said she'd be in her signature yellow dress—she wanted

to shine bright for me. That was the moment I almost called off this idiocy. She's in a different department, so when my boss suggested the date, I didn't even put it together. It's Valentine's Day. I don't celebrate Valentine's Day. Too mushy and riddled with pitfalls and potholes. I don't usually have a problem finding a date, but it felt like a good career thing to do. I'm pitching another show next week to the producers at Sirius, and thought this would help. Now I want out, or if this blue-eyed stunning girl is her, then I want in.

Traditionally I avoid cuffing season altogether. I only date from March 19th to October 12th. The smell of roses and chocolate fondue is choking me. Or it was until that fresh, beautiful face lit up when our eyes connected. She's still glancing over as if she's waiting for someone, but the way she's staring, it's like she's waiting for me. Perhaps my blind date changed her mind about the yellow. What god have I pleased for this to actually work out? It won't go past tonight. I don't date. And it's ridiculous to date a woman in this city. But what if it could be tonight with this stunning blonde in the blue dress?

I walk over, and her smile gets even more breathtaking. Seriously, no breath. Not sure I'm going to be able to say hello. She's a tractor beam pulling me towards her.

She looks eagerly as I unbutton my coat and slide it off my shoulders. Then her face falls. No. NO. I need that smile back, sexy blonde in the blue dress. Please be Tihinyho. I promise not to mock you if you're her. Please.

"Did I do something wrong already?" I speak. The brave thing reaches for my tie, and I see her slender fingers slide up and down. She's looking intently as she fingers my silk.

"Only gray. No red stripes. Not even a thin one." Her shoulders slump as she pouts and looks up at me. Looking down at her in this position has my brain going to all kinds of places it shouldn't. Damn. My cock jumps. Her lips are so close to the perfect angle to really do some damage. Why the hell is her dress blue?

I smile and slide onto the stool next to hers. "Are you ok?" She still has my tie in her hands like it's a leash. This one crackles and pops like popcorn in oil. She realizes she's still holding me and quickly removes her hand. She shakes her head, releasing a slight herbal perfume, and now I'm pretty sure I'm under some kind of voodoo spell. I turn towards her and smile. The bartender places a martini in front of her, and she puts her finger up to him.

Her voice is sultry without being raspy. "You want a drink?"

I lean on the bar and say, "What I want is world peace and a decent night's sleep, but I'll settle for a gin martini and slumming it with you."

She laughs. It's light and deep at the same time. I'm trying to be cool. I hope she thinks so, and please, for the love of my cock, let this be Melanie.

"Melanie?" I say, locking eyes with her as if I'm willing it to be so.

She exhales loudly. "Of course you're looking for someone else. Everyone always is."

She pulls the drink towards her and bends down and sips before picking it up. It's sexy and also really fucking adorable.

"Please tell me you're looking for Patrick. For the love of Eros and manufactured holidays please pretend you're looking for Patrick." She pushes the drink away from her, puts her head on the bar, and playfully taps her head on it. I laugh as she groans.

"You're not Melanie Tinywhole. I mean Tihinyho."

She laughs. "Was that a sneeze or an insult? I'm not Tinywhole—that can't be real."

"Afraid it is."

She says, "And you're sure you're not Ricky Schlong pronounced Schlein?

"Wait. We're waiting on a pussy and dick?" She laughs hard, then moans. I'm surprised cartoon steam doesn't pour out of my ears at the sound of her moan. Fuck.

"No. No. Of course I'm not looking for Patrick. I'm looking for Ricky. A grown man named Ricky, who does something in the medical field or construction but isn't a doctor or a contractor. A Ricky, my sister says, is perfect. But my sister is a shitty judge of character."

"Not interested in your sister's choices." I smile at her. She curls her lip and I want to nip at it.

"How is it you smell like a bonfire and marshmallows?" She inhales deeply.

I smirk. "I just came from a scout jamboree." She laughs, and it's bawdy and feminine.

I laugh too. She's funny. Gorgeous, sparkly, and fucking funny. No Melanie can live up to the gauntlet this woman's inadvertently thrown down.

I don't want Tihinyho when this woman is sitting all alone, and I certainly don't want her with a Ricky. Not when there's a fucking sizzle between blue dress and me. I'll tell my boss it was a missed connection. *Oh shit. I think I was at the wrong restaurant. The restaurant you told me to go to was shut down because the eels got out of the tank.* Whatever it takes. I'll text my boss and get out of this Tinywhole situation so I can get into this one. I need to get all over this blue dress, around it, behind it, and on top of it. Lots of prepositional phrases are popping into my head.

I lean on the bar to get a little closer. I say, "I'm not meeting Melanie."

She sits up straight and stares at me. "What are you saying?

Are you going to rescue me from a bad date with those light greenish eyes of yours?"

What the hell do I have to lose? It's one night, and with any luck, we can skip dinner and grab something afterward. There's a spark, heat, pull, all that bullshit, but it's all sexual. I need to lick this woman from the tip of her spiky sexy heels up to her soft honeyed hair that, if I were more of a gentleman, I'd say cascades down her neck like a waterfall. It's wavy, not curly, and it looks so soft. I'm going to touch it. I take a strand between my fingers and fuck me if even that doesn't turn me on. She bites her bottom lip. Thank Christ for this tasty little snack. She's an assortment box of chocolates of possibilities, and I'm going to have to bite each piece to see what tastes best.

12

SABRINA

I was going out with a stranger anyway but I want it to be this one. The stranger I picked. As a kid, I learned to be aggressive *and* passive—not passive-aggressive—each skill put to use to garner the most attention. I'm the middle kid. Neither here nor there in the family but both at the same time. Basically, manically all-in, or aloof and dismissive. It's not served me well romantically. My new drunken airport friends have no bias or blessing/curse of personal history with me. I raise my phone and snap a picture. He looks worried.

I look at him. "Just in case you chop me into little pieces and I go missing. The detectives will have something to go on."

He laughs. "Fair enough." He sips his drink and gives me a tiny piece of privacy. But his fucking campfire smell has me burning already.

SABRINA: Not meeting Ricky Schlong. [insert picture]. I met this guy, and we're ditching our blind dates.

TABI: Holy hot! But I'm not sure how I can go on without a picture of Ricky Schlong. My husband and other best friends are dying. We're getting day-drunk for Valentine's together. Please. Please send us a picture of Ricky Schlong.

TABI: Hey there, stranger. This is David, Tabi's very best friend in the world. So much better than her husband. This Schlong man will haunt my dreams if you don't let me see him. Please, stranger. Have mercy. I've GOT to see the Schlong.

TABI: Screw David. This is Tab's bestest of best friends, Sam. I have faith in you that you can snap a shot of the short Schlong. We're really invested in this.

TABI: Sorry about my asshole friends. But know we're all interested. And jump that hot thang in the bathroom.

SABRINA: Hopefully, I won't see him at all, but if I do, David & Sam, I promise to send one.

TRISTAN: He seems respectable. And you're all dressed up. Have a drink with him. Do not jump into the loo with him.

TABI: Prude. Why are the Brits awake?

TRISTAN: Not so much prude as someone with a bit more decorum, my dear Californian friend. And it's not that late.

TABI: Fair enough, Tris. But I'll bet you've got a freaky side.

TRISTAN: NO comment.

SABRINA: Hey! Do I do it? Do I leave with a stranger?

TABI: Where's Ben? He seems to be our voice of reason. RORY!? Are you there? Weigh in, please. Christ, Rory. Don't make us worry about you too, my international brother from another mother. Please let us know you're there. I'll never sleep if you don't check in.

JONATHAN: Sabrina, this is a possibility, I say do it. Chemistry can't be bought.

TRISTAN: Jonathan, you speak as if you're a card purchased at the chemist for your great-aunt's birthday.

TABI: Jonathan, you are such a fucking girl. Goddammit, RORY!

RORY: Be wary, Bree. Stay in public places and message at the end of the night. And Tabi, fuck off, I'm sleeping. And we are most certainly not siblings of any kind. I'd kill myself.

SABRINA: Thanks, everyone. Promise to check in later.

I place my phone on the bar and turn towards my stranger. "Patrick. I'm Sabrina." I like the way the K clicks off my tongue. He's smiling and sipping.

"You look lovely tonight, Sabrina. Dressing for other men suits you."

I grin as he lifts his martini without spilling a drop. I don't know how people do that. I'm all tingles, and cupid is slinging arrows all around. He's gorgeous. Like otherworldly gorgeous, and his eyes look kind. I hope he's not Dexter or Joe Goldberg. Who sadly are better than the men I usually end up with.

A man at the front door catches my attention. He's wearing a shiny black suit and a bright-red-striped tie. Oh god. It's like a fucking candy cane. I snap his picture and send it to the group. I nudge Patrick. He glances over my shoulder as Ricky approaches. He knows I'm wearing a blue dress. Without hesitation, Patrick wraps his arm around my waist and tugs me to standing. I'm in between his legs, and I fit perfectly in his arms. Usually, I'm like the puzzle piece you force-fit just so you can finish that section. The one jammed into the wrong spot.

He smells like cedar and sex. And like a deep, dark forest, I want to get lost in him. Seriously, I hate the outdoors, but with this man, all I can think about is camping and climbing. I grin up at him, and he's staring at my lips. I can't believe the attraction between us after like a minute. I'm not usually this girl. I'm not an impromptu gal. I'm a GPS-your-destination-from-home-before-you-get-in-the-car kind of girl.

I hear Ricky saying over and over, "Sabrina. Yo, Sabrina. Is there a Sabrina Faire here?" He's grabbing any woman in a blue dress. The manager is now involved trying to calm him down, as he whizzes around the restaurant, asking already-seated diners if they're me. My phone lights up with a text from Ricky, and his head raises at the ding. Patrick scoops up my phone and pretends to read the text, silences my ringer, then tucks my sparkly purple phone in his jacket pocket.

Ricky's making a scene. And I don't think Patrick's arm will stop him from asking who I am. I have a problem. I gesture for Patrick's ear, and he bends to me.

I whisper, "He's going to find me. I'm terrible at lying. I should go." I place my hand on his chest, and I kind of want to leave it there forever. But there's no way I'm leaving this man's arms for dinner with Ricky. I'll just take these ten perfect minutes with me as I sneak out. Patrick turns his head, and our faces are incredibly close. I can see every gorgeous, complicated fleck in his hazel green eyes. He curls his hand around mine.

He smirks and says, "Not unless you're taking me with you." Then his lips are on mine. Sure and solid. They're firm at first, as are mine in surprise, then, as he ends the slight kiss and begins another, our lips yield to each other. They fall into a gentle, playful rhythm of advancing and retreating. There's a hint of the tip of his tongue as it brushes my lips, then it's gone. This perfect stranger sweeps me up into a kiss that girls dream about. We stay in this kiss as if it's been scripted for us, and my hand moves up his chest and over to his shoulder. I never want this to end.

"Excuse me, bartender, I'm looking for Patrick Donovan."

I open my eyes with my lips still on his. There's an updo mess in an ochre dress asking about him. No, Melanie, he's with me. You're too late. I caught him like a big mouth bass. Christ, again, with an outdoor sport. To be honest, I don't know what a big mouth bass looks like. I'm hoping it has an attractive mouth.

I kiss him a little more aggressively, and he smiles into it for the briefest of seconds, then the tip of his tongue is wedging my mouth open. His date is behind him. Mine is two chairs to my left. The restaurant is full of noisy diners, but I open my mouth to him to let our tongues play a little. As I open myself to him, everything falls away except the sound of his heartbeat and the smell of the forest.

13

PATRICK

I didn't realize how lonely I was until she tugged on my tie. Valentine's Day is messing with me. Making me believe this is all more than it is. I explore her mouth until the bartender makes a noise and slides us the tab. I toss my credit card on the bill. She smiles and adjusts herself on her barstool. I take her hand and kiss the top of it.

"Can I take you to dinner?"

"That's the least of what I think you can do for me tonight." She grins and it turns my world. Her cheeks blush a bit, and it's so incredibly sexy.

I stand and help her off the stool. I hold her coat out for her.

"Thank you, Patrick." She says my name, and I want to hear it often from her lips.

"You're very welcome, Sabrina."

The voice is loud next to us, and we realize what we've done. She quickly covers her mouth.

"SABRINA? You're fucking Sabrina? Who the shit is this guy? Who the hell is Patrick? And what's he doing to my woman?" His voice rises above the din of the bar and cuts through our evening, as Melanie's head whips in our direction.

"Wait. Are you the Patrick I'm supposed to meet?"

And it's instinct. This is it after a couple of crap years. I don't want to explain. I don't want to apologize. I only want Sabrina. It's time to get what I want for the first time in my life—her. I want all of her for as long as she'll have me tonight. I can't explain it, but I need to possess her laugh, her body, her mind, and her aura. I haven't dated in a while, hooked up, sure, but dated, no. I thought this blind date might get my voice on the air more often, but something snapped the moment Sabrina pulled on my tie. I lean down into her face. She looks paralyzed and unsure of everything until she looks in my eyes, and the light switches back on for both of us.

I whisper loud enough for only her to hear, "Run."

❧ 14 ❧

SABRINA

He grabs my coat and yanks me out of the restaurant. Everyone is looking at us, and I can't stop looking back at our dates who are actually giving chase. If it were me, I would have publicly laughed it off and had a shot. But I applaud Melanie for her delusional moxie. Tinyhole and Schlong are bolting after us.

Patrick almost pulls my arm from its socket as we run down the block. It's slushy and gross, but I keep running like the Schlong has a chainsaw. I'm a champion high-heel wearer, so I'm keeping stride with his long legs that are twice the size of mine. He keeps laughing and looking back at me, and my smile joins his in lighting up the evening. I glance back, and we're starting to lose them, but they're still coming. Like they're going to catch up and somehow force us to date them.

We round the corner, and Patrick ducks into a hardware store. I trip on the threshold as he pulls me to hide behind the paint sample display.

He's above me like we're in a caper film peering around the corner of the display at the door. I whisper, "What are we doing here?"

He stands and pulls me to face him. "I'm an interior decorator and I'm on a deadline. It will just take a moment for me to pick out the new kitchen colors for the Millers." I laugh. He grabs a handful of paint color sheets without looking and shoves them in his pocket. "Done." He shrugs, and I laugh again. "They really aren't that picky."

An elderly man with a champion waxed mustache is flipping a closed sign.

"Sir," Patrick says, and he jumps and stumbles a second.

We step out. I move in front of Patrick and say, "Sir, we're sorry to startle you."

"We're closed. How the hell did you get in here?"

Patrick steps out towards him. I follow and wobble a bit. My heel is worse for wear from our marathon sprint away from the restaurant. I put my arms out and try to catch myself. I grasp one of the tiny plastic shelves full of the paint chip sheets, and as I tumble down, all the shades of blue come with me. I land hard on my butt, my legs splayed in front of me, as paint sheets tumble all around like confetti.

Patrick kneels. "You ok?" His hand is on my knee, and my skirt moves under his touch. And now my knee feels like it's scorching. He looks at me, and I get a close-up view of his eyes. I hold up a blue paint sheet to his face.

"They just turned a little blue."

He reaches around me. His face is closer to mine. The tug to kiss him is strong, but he backs up quickly. He has a mossy green paint chip and puts it near his face. "Now what do you see?"

"They're darker green. That's crazy."

"Which do you prefer?"

"I like them both." He picks up my discarded blue chips and hands me both strips.

"Then keep this safe for when you want a change tonight. You're really ok?"

"We're fucking closed. Get out," the man blusters. I smile.

"We can help pick up. I'm sorry about this," Patrick says.

The man says, "Nah. I'll make the kid do it in the morning. Now scram." I giggle as he uses scram. I bend my knee and realize we have a problem. I look at him. "The heel on my shoe is broken." I lift my leg, and it's dangling. Patrick pops up and approaches the cranky man.

"We'll get out of here as soon as I secure a strong, quick-set glue. And borrow leather snips for a moment."

I don't move from my position on the dirty-ass hardware store floor. Someone is taking care of me. That never happens. I'm the one alone and caring for myself.

My makeshift cobbler returns after following Mr. Cranky Butt around the store. Patrick places a twenty on the counter, then walks over and snips my heel off.

"Get out. That's enough." Mustache claps and points to the door.

"But I need to fix her shoe."

"Tick tock. Got Valentine's plans. If I don't get to the Elks Lodge, Marvin's gonna snake Debbie for the night. Then I'm going home alone. She's a fickle filly, and I'm not one to disappoint, so ske-fucking-daddle outta here."

Patrick takes my hand, and I stand lopsided up on one toe.

"Put your arm around me." I slide my arm around him and feel how muscular he is under his coat. The two of us almost slip again on all the paint chip strips.

"OUT!"

"Do you trust me?" he says with a wink. I shouldn't, I've known him for a blink of a time.

"As messed up as it seems, I do."

He nods at me then scoops me up into his arms. My arms go instinctively around his neck for support, and he smiles down at me.

"Get Cinderella the fuck out of here, Charming."

"My pleasure, Fairy Godfather."

"Bibbidi-bobbidi-fucking-goodnight."

He rolls his eyes, and I giggle as I put my head on his shoulder. He's warm and smells of the embers of a long night and the crisp possibility of dawn. He smells like pine needles and minerals strong enough to withstand anything. After my last year and a half, I could use someone strong enough.

The door slams as Patrick crosses the street to Central Park and sets me down on a concrete column. The whole park is lit with the full moon's reflection off the snow. The pathways have been cleared, but the park itself remains untouched and sparkles a bit under the street lights.

❧ 15 ❧

PATRICK

She's light as a wisp and smells so fucking good. She looks around and points to a bench further into the park. I scoop her back up and avoid the slush and ice. I sit next to her and pull out the glue.

"Give me your feet." She sits sideways and places her feet on my lap. I get the heel out and start to examine where it will reattach.

"Why are you being so nice to me?" She cocks her head, and her smile warms everything around us. I stare at her, a little confused by the question and totally understanding her.

"I don't know. But you're the most interesting, beautiful thing that's happened in a long while. And those damn eyes of yours, I'd probably do anything."

She smiles, and I'm still holding her legs on my lap. "You too. Your eyes. Your hands are so warm on my legs and it's comforting and natural. That's fucked up, right?"

"Here's what's going to happen."

She claps her hands like an excited seal doing a trick for a fish.

I smirk and continue, "I'm going to glue your heel on, we'll sit and wait for it to cure. Then we're finding a wonderful restaurant in this romantic city because this dress deserves dinner. We're going to laugh and get to know each other."

She inhales, and as she speaks, the condensation creates a magical cloud around her mouth. She squeezes my arm. "Yes. And can we hurry? I'm freezing." I nod. I rub my hands up and down her sparkly sheer lower legs.

I get to work drying off the bottom of her shoe. I set a two-minute timer on my phone. I put my gloves back on once I've attached the heel and hold it in place.

"What do you want to do for the next two minutes?" She bites her lip, and I want to eat her up. With my other hand, I graze her cheek with the back of my knuckle. She scoots a little closer.

She says, "You're not like other people, are you?"

"Compliment?"

"Yes. Most men at this point would have grabbed a car home and left my chaos behind. And certainly wouldn't have carried me."

I move closer to her. "I'm not most men." Her lips are rosy and full. I want to taste them again so badly. "You think you're more interesting than most women?" I grin as I tease her.

She whispers, and our faces are closer, "Oh, I am."

"Yes, but are you"—I pause to shift her legs and get a little closer to her—"interested?" We stare at each other as the chill of the night seems to create an igloo around our park bench. I glance over her shoulder and see the buildings are lit up with their hearts and red and pink lights. I hear the traffic noise, then I look at her face, and it all fades in comparison. I only hear her heartbeat and mine. This might be a bit more than lust. Dinner is usually a means to an end, but it's important tonight. I listen to her breathing catch in excitement and anticipation. I slowly move towards her lips.

Beep. Beep. Beep.

I'm startled and pull back, and she shakes her whole body like a chill invaded her soul. The moment's gone, and I can't get that lost kiss back. The cold and chilly reality of us sitting on a park bench in fucking February takes hold.

"Time's up. Let's see how we did?" I let go, and she suddenly lifts her leg straight into the air, giving a lovely view of her calf, but as she does, the heel seems to be holding on. I feel it slip off my hand, and we both stare at her leg in the air.

"Shit." Dangling off her shoe is my glove.

She laughs at the sight of it. "Would you kindly remove your glove?"

I take her legs off me and stand up. She's still on the bench, and now her shoe is at eye level with me. I grab her ankle, and I swear I hear her gasp at the exact moment my dick stirs. It's a very lovely ankle. Without thinking, I kiss her sparkly almost sheer tights and grab my glove. But as I tug, it won't come off.

"Fuck."

"What?" She lowers her feet to the ground and sits up. My glove is glued to the bottom of her shoe. The black leather glove fills with air as she lowers her foot, then slams it to the ground. "You're kidding?"

"I don't know how that happened. I'm so sorry. I know how to glue things. I've won awards in gluing." I'm vamping. "I can fix this." I'm panicking a bit. I look like a moron in front of the goddess of a woman I'm trying to impress. Shit. I squat down and realize there are three glove fingers attached to the shoe. I try to wedge my fingers under the leather and work it free. "Hold on." She grips the bench, and I pull incredibly hard. My fist slides off the glove and bashes into my own eye. Everything pinches in my brain for a moment as I fall on my ass. Now, I'm sitting in salty slush and it's seeping into my pants. I quickly pop up. My eye is killing me.

"Holy fuck. Fuck that hurt."

"Oh my god." She jumps off the bench and tries to walk on her heels. There's a slight limp because one is so much taller than the other now, and she's dragging my glove. I walk around blinking, trying to get my vision back. And now my eye stings like a mutha because I have some of the salty slush on my hand, and I put it in my fucking asshole eye.

"I'm fine. Totally fine. This is all under complete control. I have a plan. No worries." The fact she's not limp running away from me is a miracle. As I squint, I see her break an icicle from the bench and put it into her woollen glove. Now she rescues me. She places the scratchy soggy glove on my eye, and the cool ice soothes. When my mom sat me down for one of her 'talks' one time, she said someday someone will turn the light on for me. That I wouldn't notice when it happened, only that I'm no longer in the dark. Then I'd know I'm no longer alone. I thought she was talking about my dad, but that wasn't true. I figured it was a myth. But now, even if it's only for the next six hours, it's nice not to feel alone.

When I open my other eye, she's crooked. I hope it's the shoes that took my vision and the world off its axis.

She says, "I'm getting weak from hunger and if I have to drag a glove around all night, I'm going to need food for strength." She grins, and even that is a little crooked and thoroughly fucking charming.

16

SABRINA

I t's nearly nine as we clomp towards dinner. My glove is on his eye, and his is on my shoe. There's an odd symmetry to it. This man with my glove on his eye is lovely. He's not perfect, but he is. Does that even make sense? I'm flying on gut instinct. I know how to be aggressive but not bold. Perhaps my new friend, Tabi, is rubbing off on me. I want to be bold enough to be in the moment with this unexpected Valentine's gift. I take his extended hand. "To food."

We walk across the street to a bustling bistro. He squeezes my hand, and I keep trying to scrape off the glove by scuffing it along the ground. Sadly now it's wet and there are pebbles stuck to it, like a mini leather albatross. I'm trying to walk straight, but the shoes really are different heights and angles now.

"How's your eye?"

"Fine. How's my glove?"

I giggle. "Fine."

He leans to me and kisses the side of my head, and now I fucking want him. A simple touch of his lips and my entire body is glowing. I'm a lightning bug's butt. We're bonded by diversity. Like we've conquered something. He holds open the door. His eye is a little puffy, but I won't say a word.

"Good evening, do you have a reservation?" a pert woman says.

I say, "I'm sorry we don't. And we've had a hell of a night. We'd love to sit at the bar and eat if that's possible. Or take any cancellation you might have."

The woman smiles sweetly at us. "You do know it's Valentine's Day?"

I say, "We do. And it's a very long story. We did have a table somewhere but..."

He tucks me into his side and turns towards her, so she sees his slightly puffy eye. I thought for a moment he was going to mansplain the situation but then I see he's just feeding this woman what she wants. His chiseled jaw, his perfect hair, the light stubble, and those gleaming green hazel eyes. The son of a bitch is going to flirt and lean in to his black eye for sympathy. He smiles at the woman, and she's trapped in his gaze. It's almost too much to watch his charm work on someone else.

"What's your name?"

She actually fucking blushes. "Robin."

"Lovely," he mutters purposely under his breath as if she's catching him admiring her. Damn, he's fucking good. "Robin, as you can see, we're worse for the wear. We literally ran away from our other dates to be together tonight. They chased us and we were injured, and now they're sitting at our table at Crain's." She smiles and licks her lips. Tuck your fucking lips back, missy. I'm scrappy tonight and willing to fight for him. He nods and says, "I need you to be our Cupid, Robin. And

I'm sorry you have to work tonight. I'm sure there's someone waiting for you to get off work."

"No. Not this year." She tucks her hair behind her ear.

"The world's loss." I'm pretty sure she's going to toss her panties at him in a second. She's cornered by his charm. "Can you help us out?"

She goes to her tablet and starts to move things around. He whispers, "You do know you're different, right?" That floods over me and warms me up. He squeezes me to his side, and there's that fucking zing between us again. Almost like when someone plucks a wire that's too taut. I snuggle into him and get another whiff of that campfire, and again I want to live in a tent in the middle of nowhere with this man.

She smiles at him, and her eyes dance, but his don't. Thank god. "May I have your phone?" He fishes his phone out of his jacket and hands it to her, then hands me mine, which I forgot he had. I can't look at anything except his long fingers and large beautiful hands. Her hot-pink nails graze his finger as she hands it back to him. A slight noise erupts from me, and he looks down at me. He grins and goes to my ear. "Did you just growl at her?"

I shake my head. I'm mortified. Did I growl at her?

He trails his hands up and down mine. "No need to pull out the claws, I'm yours tonight, no questions or doubts." He brushes his lips over the shell of my ear, and those damn goosebumps pop up all over my body. He sucks on the itty-bitty spot just behind my ear and purrs, "Are you mine?" I turn my head and look at him—his eyes are dancing. That's right, Robin. I make his eyes dance. He says louder, "Are you, tonight?"

"Very much so."

His arm squeezes me closer. He's ducking down to get in my face for a moment. "Soon, I hope. Christ, I hope soon." And his eyes flick upwards. I grin uncontrollably and nod. I'm happy skipping dinner. I leave early tomorrow morning to go back to Chicago, and I want tonight with him to be as long as possible. I'd like to manipulate time like Hermione, and have him so many times we lose track of days, but I also want to sit across from him. I want to know him.

Robin interrupts our eye fucking. "Ok. You'll have a tight hour to eat. I'll text you and you have to sit down right away. Don't wander."

"That's fantastic, darling Robin. Thank you so much." He winks. We head to the bar. He reaches into his wallet to give his card to the bartender.

"Shit."

"What?"

"I left my card at the other bar." He slams his hand onto the bar. And his charming side cracks a tiny bit. I like it. Fall apart, Mr. Perfect. I'm a mess. Join me.

I put my hand on his forearm. "It's ok. Let's go get it. I'm sure we have time. You slink in and get it. And if we have to abandon the mission, I'll buy dinner." Without warning, he slams his lips on mine, and my arms go around his neck. He's so yummy.

"I couldn't wait another fucking second to taste you again."

His tongue sweeps into my mouth, and I plaster my body to him, even though we're still wearing coats. I can feel how much he likes me on my hip. I pull my head away for a second, and he shakes his and he's on my lips again. It's strong and sexy and everything. His long fingers splay out on my back, molding me to him. Our kiss has a story of its own. It's fevered and then deep and interesting and then light and soft. Then over.

"You're so fucking great. Easy," he says as if incredulous.

"Whore easy or laid-back easy?"

He laughs. "Both. I'm thrilled to find out you're a funny and intelligent slut. Makes it worth putting on pants and leaving the house." I slap his arm. "Come on, my beautiful whore." I like being his. I like it too much. Every word he says has a crackle and a promise to it. Like everything out of our mouths is essential. I feel treasured.

I hobble down the street and snake my hand up his arm, pulling myself closer. He exhales and leans his head down onto mine. It's as close as we can get fully clothed and walking. We pass a group of restaurant workers smoking and bitching about the clientele. I used to wait tables, it's very familiar.

He pulls me to him suddenly. "I know we have to hustle but I need your lips."

I grin. "I need yours too."

He places his hands on either side of my face and slowly the kiss unfolds. He slides a hand into my hair, and I'm fucking floating on chemistry and lust. He increases the pressure and moans a little. Then he pulls his head back. "I'm hot."

I kiss him again. "Me too."

He jerks himself away from me. "NO. I'm hot." He begins spinning, like a dog trying to catch its tail. "I'm fucking smoking."

I bend down and see a flicked cigarette butt stuck in the cuff of his pants. He's still spinning wildly.

"Stop fucking moving, you're fanning the flames!"

"Flames! I'm on fucking fire?!!"

I bend over, and the wind throws my dress up over my head, but I swat wildly at the ember with my purse as it burns a hole through his pants. "Oh my god. Oh my god. Stop freaking moving."

He stops. "Your ass is spectacular, side note. Now, put the fucking fire out."

I'm hitting his leg. "Stop squirming." My ass is freezing as I'm on display for everyone on 7th Avenue. I smash my hand against his Achilles. He holds my dress down, but I can feel the panic in his hands as I swat my purse at his leg.

"STOP GRINDING A LIT CIGARETTE INTO MY FUCKING ANKLE." I'm laughing and hitting. "Jesus. Is it out?" It's just smoking now, and I pick it out of his pants and toss it away from us.

"It's out. Shit. Are you ok?" I pop up into his face and rearrange my dress and coat.

He throws his hands in the air. "I'm totally cool." His face is all screwed up. "I was on fucking fire, what do you think?"

I bite the inside of my cheek.

He bends down, pulls his pant leg around, and examines the burnt hole. Then lifts his pant leg and tries to see. There's a small burn. I can smell the burnt hair. "Is it bad?" I shake my head. "I mean, do we need to go to urgent care?" he asks earnestly, and I cannot believe this.

"That's my dream date. Swoon." I put the back of my hand to my forehead.

"Seriously, Sabrina, can you look?" Oh my god, he's one of those men who can't handle a common cold. I grin at him. I'll continue teasing him later. I bend down holding my dress down, and lift his pant leg to examine. It's a small slightly red mark. I lean to his calf, lick the "burn", then kiss it gently. Then begin to slowly kiss it again as sensually as I can. He starts laughing, then smacks my ass. I stumble forward but catch myself.

"Ok, funny girl. And fuck me with the thigh highs. Jesus you're insanely sexy even with that hell of bruise blooming on your thigh. Is that from the hardware store?"

"My ass was exposed to the world, and you're worried about a bruise, that's both sweet and disappointing. I thought my ass was—"

He interrupts with a desperate fevered kiss and squeezes my ass intensely.

"Your ass is fucking everything. But if we're going to get through dinner, I need to focus on something other than those peaches and cream cheeks and that small scarlet lace strip separating me from what I imagine is the most perfect pussy ever."

I gasp. "That's better. Was anything else injured in the fire? I can kiss it better."

He grabs me closer and my breath catches. "I have other aching parts, but first we grab my credit card, get back here and eat. Then, I will eat you. But the burn fucking hurts."

My whole body lights up. "Really?"

I put my hand on his chest and smirk at him. Then he's on my lips before I can say anything else.

❧ 17 ❧

PATRICK

This woman, taking the piss out of me. She says, as we begin to walk, "Did you just kiss me so I'd stop teasing you."

"Perhaps. Did it work?"

"For now. But we'll need to hurry if we're going to make your appointment at the burn unit." I walk towards the restaurant, but she doesn't stop mocking. "Let's pop into CVS and grab gauze and maybe book some time in a hyperbaric chamber. You'll be good as new."

She hugs me and wiggles under my arm. I pretend to ignore her.

She keeps talking, "We got this. I'll be right by your side during the skin graft." I burst into laughter and try not to look at her. She continues, "I'm going nowhere during this tragedy. For better or worse." There's a zing through my nervous system, and my spine stiffens for a moment. I try to relax without her noticing.

There's an awkward silence for the first time. Those were jarring words. I just met this woman. Slow your roll, Sabrina. I exhale, and she sighs. This sucks. We walk in silence, and she loosens her grip on my waist and attempts to step away from me. As she does, a rush of cold air surges and touches the exact spot she's left. I pull her back to my side and kiss the top of her head. That's odd. That was a reflex. I don't want her to be anywhere but close. I have a touch of whiplash as I try to figure out what it all means. I don't need anyone in my life except my brothers. That's the way I'm designed, but this mysterious little minx has my head reeling. Who else does she tease? Who else has she run away with? I want a list, then I want some time to hunt those men down. Your turn, Patrick— time to slow your roll.

I wrap my left arm around her and hold her close. We walk lopsided down the street to the sound of her crooked heel and a scrap of my glove still attached to it.

After a block, I say, "For better or worse, huh?"

She looks up at me, and her blue eyes liquefy my insides. They're my salvation and my ruin. "I'm not one of those fair-weather one-night stands. I'll see my commitments through until dawn." She steps back, kisses three fingers, crosses her heart, and holds them up like a Girl Scout pledge. I grin. No one makes me laugh. That's my job. I'm the joker, and certainly, no one teases me. I try to beat everyone to the punch before they can find a flaw. I'll point it out first. This creature is everything. It might not be the worst thing if she sees the worst.

"I was worried you were one of those women who's only in this until 11 p.m. I mean if you can't stick it out until dawn, what's even the point?" She smiles, and I kiss her quickly, then put my forehead to hers. "Now. The restaurant is just up ahead, what's the game plan, gorgeous?"

"Is that my pet name?"

"Not good?"

"Could use some work, seems generic." She grins as I slide my hand into her golden hair.

"There is nothing generic about you." She pulls my scarf to bring me closer, but that's not something she needs to do. She has me completely tonight. I want to get swept up in the lust and the idea that this is my girl.

My card can wait. My dick can't. I guide her to the building next door. There's an abandoned tiny tented vestibule and large planters full of flowers and white lights arranged for Valentine's Day. It's as private as I need for this moment. It's like we're standing in one of those old-timey striped Atlantic City changing rooms on the beach. Her eyes flash desire. I take her lips, and she instantly exhales and moves closer. My hand is grasping at the buttons on her coat, and she's opening my scarf. I tug her jacket open and finally get to see the blue dress again. This sapphire dress screams to be left on the floor by my bed. She pulls back and smiles.

"Patrick. This is"—I take my hands off her and raise an eyebrow, curious where she's going with this—"fucking crazy. It's nuts how much I want you. I don't even know you, but I feel like we're war buddies at this point."

I put my forehead to hers. "Your foxhole or mine?" My hand goes up to her thigh and I play with the elastic top of her thigh highs. She gasps, then smiles. Her skin is so soft and inviting. I skate my hand over her inner thigh, and she bites her lip. I want to rent space between her legs for an extended vagina vacation.

I skim my hand closer to where I'm destined to be, and she moves into me, searching for friction and release. My cock is rock hard at the thought of hitching her on my hips and bouncing her up and down until we both shatter the sound barrier with our grunts and screams. Our lips don't leave each other. We keep inventing new hot-as-fuck ways to kiss each other. Fuck. My dick is insanely hard. Her hand moves to my pants, and she finds her way just inside my waistband and ghosts the tip.

"Fuck, woman. You're so hot. I need to touch you right fucking now. I need to make sure you're mine tonight."

"Um, yes. Stop teasing and get in my foxhole." I laugh and move my hand slightly away, and she groans. Then I lightly creep my fingertips up and push one finger just inside what I know is red lace. She moans. Next, I move my fingers up and down her slit brushing her clit lightly.

I move to her ear and nip slightly. "Beautiful Sabrina, you're quite wet. Even in this cold I can feel your warmth coat my fingers. After being such a naughty girl and dragging my glove through the streets tonight, is this how you plan to keep my hand warm?" I rim her, then push the pad of my finger slightly inside her and out again.

"Fuck, yes. That. Do more of that." I push my thumb to her clit as I thrust two fingers quickly inside of her. She's so wet and perfect. Her voice is rough and raw. "That. Patrick. That."

"This? Will this make you come for me? I want to see and feel you come for me, gorgeous Sabrina." Then I pull my hand out completely.

Her eyes are wild and dark with lust, as I'm sure mine are. She paws at me, attempting to get me back inside her. She loses her balance on the jacked-up heel. She clutches at me and almost falls through our makeshift shelter. The whole thing sways and creaks. I grab her just before she lands. She looks at me like I'm dipping her in some ridiculous ballroom dance. She laughs, and it's literally a noise that brightens my soul. I want to hear it all the time.

"No more disasters!" I grin and lean her against a planter, away from the structure. The flowers and little lights are framing her face, and she's breathtaking. I kiss her lightly, and she moans, then groans. I cock an eyebrow.

My phone vibrates in my pocket, and she jumps back.

"No worries." It vibrates again. She smiles that knowing grin I'm coming to really like. I ignore my phone and brush my lips over hers. She shakes her beautiful blonde hair and I pull a piece off of her lips. Then she kisses me, and it's lusty and perfect. She moans, and I bite her bottom lip and tug a bit.

"Ouch. Fuck. Ouch."

I pull back. I didn't mean to cross a line.

I glance at her, and her hand and the side of her face are suddenly red and springing welts.

❦ 18 ❦

SABRINA

He steps away and looks to the sky. "That is quite enough, universe. I was about to finger the most perfect foxhole I've come across in my vast experience. What the fuck? Can we please stop fucking with my night?! That's enough! Is this penance for the Schlong?!" Then he turns back to me quickly. "Are you ok?"

No. This cannot be happening. I don't have an EpiPen. Fuck. My eye tingles. Swelling shut is its next trick. I can feel the allergic reaction skate across my exposed skin. I'm only allergic to one fucking thing. In the universe. One fucking thing. My lip is swollen, and my eyes are watering.

He looks horrified, and I've just lost his attention for the night. I turn and look at the planter. It's been decorated with flowers for Valentine's Day, and it's covered with Queen Anne's Lace. I didn't notice it before. I didn't think I'd have to. Who decorates with a fucking spring and summer weed in the middle of winter in downtown Manhattan?

"Allergic." I step away from the flowers and point to the offending lacey piece of shit. My face is beginning to itch, and my hand has raised bumps. My mouth is starting to resemble a carp, and he looks panicked.

He *is* panicked. "Hospital?! Do you need a hospital? Was it the flowers?"

"You can go." I need to be alone. He can't see me turn into a mottled strawberry. My lips are stinging and the welts on my hand are spreading. I can feel them. "The white ones. Not standard in winter. I have to get to a drug store." I turn, and he pulls me back. And realizes he probably has the offending piece of shit fake flower all over him. "Now."

He pulls out his phone and points down the block. "Duane Reed is around the corner. Come on."

I protest, "No, you don't have to. I'm so gross right now."

He stops in front of me, careful not to touch me. "Stop it. You're still gorgeous even when you resemble a lychee." I groan. This can't be happening. "Come on, Hives. That can be your pet name, Hives." I try to smile but can't close my mouth. And here comes the drool.

He leads the way, and I try to keep up with one eye now shut, my wobbly uneven heels, and drool sliding involuntarily down the left side of my face, like I've been numbed with novocaine.

"Waith." Oh fuck. Now my tongue has joined this carousel of pain and humiliation. He doesn't hear me. "WAITH. WAITH. Mya heelz ith too unebenen."

He turns around. "Did you just say—holy shit, SABRI-NA!" He doesn't hesitate; he scoops me up and throws me over his shoulder in a fireman carry. My ass cheek is bouncing in his face cheek, and all the blood is rushing to my scratchy, bumpy, and swollen face. He's in an all-out run. For the second time in a couple of hours, the man is carrying me. He's strong. I mean, like surprisingly strong. He bursts through the doors.

"EpiPen now!!! I'll pay whatever the cost. Now!"

I smack his back, and he puts me down on my unstable feet. I move out of the way as a twenty-year-old terrified drug store employee lunges at me with a needle. I put a hand up and shake my head no. "Noth. Dought. Waith!" I manage to say.

He says, "Slow your roll there, drugstore cowboy." The kid flumps onto the floor. I leave them. I'm on a mission.

I wobble down the aisle, rip open a bottle of kids' liquid Benadryl, and start chugging. I'm probably going to be kiddie high any minute, but at least I won't look like I went toe to toe with a fucking beehive. I slide down to the floor, and he crouches in front of me. I can feel the medicine working its fairy-dust magic to transform me back to me, instead of the Swamp Thing.

"Dwo not wet me dink endyting." He grins and leans against the family planning section. He reaches up and tosses me a box of condoms. I smile as best I can. "Sdill? Yood till tuck me?"

He laughs very hard, then says, "I'm so relieved. And I can't wait to tuck you all night. I can't wait to tuck you until you can't take anymore tucking. My dick is down to tuck." My lips are still a touch like Lisa Rinna's lips, but they're starting to feel like my own.

He smiles and gestures for my bottle of Benadryl. "Come on, let me have a swig." I pull my mouth into a grimace of sorts.

He jumps to his feet and pulls me up. He turns on his heels, and I follow him as he heads to the cleaning section. He opens a pack of baby wipes and Clorox wipes. He wipes down his hands, his coat, and my jacket. He throws away his remaining glove, then disappears. He comes back with makeup remover and nail scissors. He bends down and cuts the bulk of his glove off my shoe, then stands and wipes his whole face with a wipe. Then he gently wipes off my cheeks and lips. He's careful around the eye area. I'm sure my mascara is streaking down my cheeks.

"There you are." He kisses me ever so slightly. It's tingly and perfect.

"Thank you. I have trouble swallowing pills. I usually carry around a bottle of the kid stuff in the summer but I never imagined I'd need it now."

"Are you sure you're ok?"

"Yes. I'm fine. Thank you. I'll be red for a while." He holds me and gets close.

"Your tongue seems back to normal. Shall we test it out?" I grin and nod. He slides his tongue against mine. I know he can taste the synthetic grape of the children's medicine. It's soft at first, just teasing, then our tongues find their rhythm. I want to be horizontal with this man very soon. His phone buzzes again.

"I should probably look at that." He glances down. "Fuck."

"Is everything ok?"

"We missed our table and we're never welcome there again. Good thing Manhattan is full of restaurants because I'm plowing through them tonight."

"I'm starving," I whine.

"Come on, I'm going to get you fed. I promise. And then, whether you like it or not, I'm going to need to see those breasts. They've been bottled up in that coat for so long tonight. I worry they don't know how much I'm going to appreciate them. They're in the dark without my mouth to gratify them."

I smile. "They really do need some air—it's kind of you to consider them."

He starts collecting our various open packages, leaving the used things on the ground in a discarded plastic bag. "I'm an empath. I sense even the slightest bit of suffering." He puts his hand on my back and guides me towards the counter.

He reaches for his wallet. "FUCK. My credit card."

I nod. "I've got all this, go get your card. Surely Ricky and Melanie are done."

He kisses my forehead. "You're still blotchy, but cute. If he's in there, anything you want me to tell the Schlong?"

I smile. "See if he's available for St. Patrick's Day."

Patrick narrows his eyes at me. "That's my holiday." He wags a finger at me. "Meet me out front. Wish me luck."

"You don't need luck, it's your credit card."

He shrugs and tosses a Beanie Boo at me as he exits. I buy the stupid white bear with creepy wide eyes. It's holding a pink heart, and someone at the factory decided its name is "Kismet."

19

PATRICK

I don't know anything about her. I don't know where she works or lives. I wrap my scarf around my neck as I head back around the corner to Ricky's restaurant. That's what it will forever be in my mind. But, wait, I take that back. I do know something about her. She's funny. She's gorgeous and kind. She's a caretaker but doesn't take shit from me. She's playful and game for anything so far. Sabrina's been dragging my glove all night without a complaint. And then there's the way she makes me feel. I don't have to pretend to be someone else. I do that in my everyday life. My DJ persona is just that, a persona. No one has taken the time to just be with me in a long time. I'm always the one driving a conversation or making the joke, but tonight we shared all of it. She kept up with me at every step. I never questioned my desire to kiss her, even though she was still blotchy and mottled from her reaction.

No one has ever made me feel cared for like this, like not

only my opinion matters but my thoughts. I'm not worried about being figured out or discovered a fraud because somehow, in the most fucked up way, she already knows the important parts of me. The rest of it all is simply facts and details.

Just as I reach for the door, I hear her clomping unsteadily up the street. I turn, and the streetlights hit her face; it's still a little red but stunning. I have no clue how to see her past tonight. It's fucking impossible, but Christ, do I want to.

I spin around, stomp, and jump up and down. She's staring at me with one heel higher than the other, wrapping her coat around herself. "I'm sure I'm going to be struck by lightning. There's not a cloud in the sky, but if there was, it would fucking cocksucking find one of us. Fuck me. Enough with the disaster."

I stare at her. She cocks one of her sexy hips and says, "It's your turn, you take the lightning. I mean, you already have the burns."

I rush to her and take her face in my hands. "Please don't run away. Whatever the fuck this is, we have to be disaster proof at this point. You're the novelty of my life right now. The thing I never expected but always wanted. You're dessert for dinner."

She grins, and it's stunning.

I continue, "You're my white whale. You're a unicorn, riding a mermaid, singing a siren song that only I can hear while the Bears win a Super Bowl."

She nods and says, "Disaster proof," then leans in and kisses me.

I shake my head, not understanding how I got this fucking lucky, finding this insanely perfect person to be on this bizarre adventure with. "I'm getting my credit card, then we're scarfing down whichever food we find first. Then we're going to find a bed and I'm going to tuck you like you've never been tucked before."

"You really do know how to wine and dine a gal."

"My version is a little different, it's children's Benadryl and street meat." She nods. I don't like people for this long. I don't want women around me longer than it takes to convince them to suck my dick. But I can't get enough of this one. She giggles as I tiptoe into the restaurant and bend down as if I'm cartoon sneaking in.

She stands out front. I'm slinking to the bar, hoping to snag the card. The bartender nods at me. Thank fucking god. Now we can grab a hot dog or something. Maybe she can cook me something. I hold my card and nod to the man. He brings me the receipt to sign, and I tip the hell out of him. I finish signing, and my elbow is pulled. Ricky's arm is cocked. Why the hell is he still here?

A woman at the bar says to her friend, "Ooo. Is this the guy? Is this Patrick the woman stealer?" I look at her for a split second, and the moron punches me. He misses my face and slams my shoulder. Really?

"Settle down, Schlong," I say. The entire restaurant giggles, and he turns his bloated red face to the room.

"It's pronounced SHLEEEN. It's a very popular and historical name in Wisconsin. It has a long and storied past." And fucking Tinywhole is still here too. What the fuck? Melanie is flailing her arms, wailing no one loves her in the corner. It's a madhouse as Ricky lectures on his last name. I slip towards the door. Ricky stops, leaps the three steps down and lands before me. Then he bends over as if he's pulled a hammie.

"Goddamn gout." I bite my tongue, and Sabrina enters. Her eyes pop wider, and she buries her giggle in her scarf. We both shake from trying not to laugh. The manager is dealing with

Melanie, who is shrieking for some reason, and points to the door.

I try to defuse the situation. Ricky stands between Sabrina and me. I put my hands up. "Hey, man. I'm sorry the night went down like this, but calm the fuck down."

"Fuckers like you think you can—"

I shake my head and try to walk around him. I just want to dive face-first into his blind date's pussy. Leave me the fuck alone, Schlong. I get to the other side of him, but he yanks my elbow back, and I flinch. I yank my arm from him, elbowing him rather hard. Then I shove him away. The moment gets me.

I say, "Don't make me end this, Schlong." The idiot dramatically stumbles backward. The entire restaurant is looking. I see a huge man stand up, groaning, and make his way over to us. Ricky yells and spins around the space, "You all saw that. He fucking attacked me."

"Come on," I whine. You're kidding. The manager is standing with Ricky and looking him over to see if there's damage of any sort, then scowls at the two of us.

"I can end this," Ricky blusters.

"Christ. Give it the fuck up, Schlong."

"SCHLEEN!" Melanie screeches behind me.

The giant man looks at me. "You are going to need to make this up to my wife. But you did hit him, and I saw it. And now I'm obligated. So, son, I'm sorry, but you have the right to remain silent—"

Sabrina yells, "What are you doing?!"

"Ma'am, I need to arrest your boyfriend for assault and battery."

She doesn't miss a beat. "Of course, you do. Because there's no lightning. Arrest away, officer. We'll figure this out too." She throws her arms in the air. I smile at her.

Ricky pokes me. "See, muthafucker, that's what you get. That's what you get for stealing another man's woman."

"You never met her before!" He pokes me again.

The officer says, "Sir, please step back. I have this handled. Go back to your evening. And keep it down, the restaurant has been through enough." Then the nice policeman puts his hand on my arm and leads me out as the restaurant claps.

20

SABRINA

Two hours of uncomfortable plastic, the municipal smell of Pine-Sol and pencil shavings. It's 12:48 when the arresting officer walks towards me.

"You ok, there?" His face is kind and he looks exactly how you want a cop to look like, as if he cares and doesn't take any shit.

I nod. "Sir, please tell your wife we're so sorry that Ricky—"

"Schlong?" The man purses his lips and shakes his head.

"It's pronounced Schlein."

The officer bursts into a giant belly laugh, and so do I. Tears run down our faces as we keep trying to compose ourselves. I say, "And her last name was Tinywhole."

The officer puts his hand up. "Stop. Please. No." He's bent over laughing with his arms out like he's blocking defenders.

"Pronounced Tinhinyho."

"Aw, shit." He can barely speak. We laugh as if we're

releasing all the tension in the world. Finally, the officer walks around breathing to calm himself. I wipe my eyes.

"Patrick only wanted to be with me tonight. He, Schlong, was my blind date."

He nods. "I figured it all out. Manager kicked them out. He apologizes for misreading the situation. He complained Patrick stole something precious. Once Mr. Schlein"—a giggle escapes his lips—"calmed down, he admitted to messing up everyone's night."

"Sweet Jesus. Patrick can leave?" He shifts his weight and smiles. "Is there somewhere to grab food? We missed all the dinners."

He places his hand on my shoulder. "The way he keeps asking about you is sweet. You make a lovely couple."

"I only met him tonight."

"Not by the way the two of you act. You met somehow somewhere along the timeline. You act like my wife and I do. Anticipating each other's moves and phrases, and eyes always searching for the other one in a room."

I swallow hard. He hands me a twenty-dollar bill. "Dinner's on me. Vending machine is back there in the breakroom. He's alone in his holding cell, I'll clear it for you to visit."

"Thank you." I hug the giant man. He pats my head, and I release him.

"Happy day after Valentine's Day." He winks at me and leaves the building. I pull my slightly tattered dress into place and wipe the remains of my eyeliner and mascara from under my eyes. I pull my hair into a chignon at the base of my neck and secure it with a pen. I apply a touch of lip gloss, and now I feel ready for my Valentine's Day date.

. . .

I PILE ALL THE VENDED PRESERVATIVE-LADEN GOODIES INTO an evidence bag along with one of those scratchy blankets cops always seem to have to soothe the victim in movies.

We round the corner, and he's sitting on the floor in the middle of the cell with his head in his hands. I'm sure if there were other people around, he would've been joking and laughing to hide away himself. But I see he's upset. I place my hand on the officer's arm and put my finger over my lips. He smiles and leaves.

I sing loudly, "Hoh ah, hoh ah. That's the sound of the men. Working on the chain gang..." He leaps to his feet. His face is framed by the bars as his hands go to hold them. I stand in the middle of the room and put my hands on my hips. His eyes light up the entire room. My whole body is squirmy and warm, simply being around him. Having his intense gaze on me is everything I could have dreamed of tonight. His charcoal shirt is pulling across a taut chest, and his sleeves have been rolled up, giving a peek of a tattoo on his forearm dusted with dark hair. His tie is gone. Still standing about six feet from him, I cock my head to the side trying to get a look at his ass. He smiles and turns around slowly. I take in his long legs and see the burn hole in the back of his pants. He pauses and clenches his ass for me, and I laugh. Then, when his eyes are on me again, he puts his finger in the air and twirls it. I do a slow turn for him. When my back is to him, he hisses low and sexy. I clench my ass cheeks, and he chuckles. I turn back around and smile at him smiling at me.

"Is this a conjugal visit?" I laugh hard and shake my head a little. He's so damn funny. "Why are you here? I thought you'd be long gone."

"Ricky cancelled on me. I had time to kill."

He beckons me with a crook of his finger. "Come here." I

set my goods down on the chair and walk over to the metal bars.

"I'm here." I get as close to him as I can.

"And thank god for that."

His hand reaches for mine, and the touch is electric, and not just because I have a prison fantasy brewing in my brain. I kiss him through the jail bars—we can't kiss the way I'd like, but it's a jolt of affirmation. It says all the things I was prepping to tell him, all the words that would rush out if I gave them a chance.

"I don't want to be anywhere else," I say.

He squeezes my hand and looks at me with an intensity that could cut through a crowd but is only meant for me.

"I'd like to be somewhere else. Kind of anywhere but jail." I laugh again. His lips curl a little up to the right, and I see his slightly puffy light green eye. His cobbler war wound. He's still hot as fuck. I'm not that special, yet this man treats me like I'm precious, perfect, and his.

If someone gave me a catalogue of all the men in the world, I could flip through and pick. I'd choose him—every time. And even if it's only for one night, I choose him. I don't know how to tell him I'm leaving tomorrow.

21

PATRICK

"Well, there's one place I'd like to be more than any other."

"Where?"

"Between your thighs, but alas, I'm going to have to pay my debt to society first." I see her shift her weight as desire settles in the exact place I just described. Fuck, I want to give her that relief.

"What if I told you I have two surprises?"

"Besides you and the fact I ended my Valentine's Day in jail?"

She spreads a blanket at the edge of my cell. I mean, what the fuck is this night? As she sits, her dress gaps a little. I get a hint of a delicious lace bra that matches that scrap covering my future destination. I exhale and sit across from her.

"I have a picnic and they're processing you. The manager got the story from the sexy bartender." What the fuck? I sit ramrod straight, and she giggles.

"Did you fuck the bartender while I've been inside?"

She laughs and flexes her fingers as her royal blue eyes knock me off my game. "Life had to go on." I would fucking rip that guy apart.

She says, "I did crosswords and scrolled social media on a hard plastic chair, while I pined for my man and kept the home fires burning." She laughs at her own joke.

I swell with pride even though it's a joke. I know this all ends in a couple of hours, but for the first time in my life, I genuinely want to be someone's man. I'm not sure I'm up to the task, but I could give it a shot. She makes me want to be worthy.

"The manager felt terrible he misread the situation."

I cross my legs and scoot closer to my bars. The floor is cement, and I'm sure it's caked in urine. I imagine every surface in here is caked in piss. My fucking pants are ruined. I glance down at my feet and remember they're already destroyed from when I was set on fire and landed in a dirty puddle in the park.

I look at her shoe, still crooked with the remnants of my glove shredded on it. Her hair's messy, her makeup is stale, and there's a stubborn blotch on her neck. But her lip gloss looks fresh, which is adorable. If this is the way I remember her in the future, I'll only ever think of her as stunning.

"You're incredible," I say.

"Because I can work a vending machine?"

I grin and reach for her hand.

"Yes. I think that makes you a tech genius. I'll bet you're in charge of something. You decide fates."

Her eyes light up. "I do! I award college scholarships!"

"You DO make the world a better place by giving away someone else's money. Guess what I do." She never will. No one ever does, unless I begin to geek out over music and we've barely had time to talk between disasters.

"You use your humor and charm to convince people of things."

I grin. I do. "I'm a DJ."

"Wedding/Bar Mitzvahs?"

"I focus more on sweet-sixteen parties and golden anniversaries." For the first time tonight, I think I got her. She looks super skeptical.

"No. Really?"

I shake my head, and her laugh takes over the room. "No. I have a show on the Spectrum channel of Sirius Satellite radio. It runs nine to midnight, Monday through Friday." She squeezes my hand, and our eyes lock again. We're staring at each other like idiots, but I can't look away.

"What's for dinner, honey?" She presents a Sprite and a Mountain Dew Major Melon. "What am I looking at?"

"The only pop left in the machine." I grin as she says "pop." That's a midwestern thing. It might be too hard for me to learn any more of her details.

"What the fuck is Mountain Dew Major Melon?" I reach my hand out. "Let me be the gentleman and drink the mysterious, unpopular but still available, pop."

"How chivalrous."

"Do you still have Benadryl? We don't know what the fuck is in this, I might convulse." I laugh at my joke as she dumps the bright multicolored bounty onto the blanket handing me KitKats, Cool Ranch Doritos and turkey jerky.

"You need protein."

"Do I?"

She winks and bites her bottom lip. I want to rip the bars open like a gorilla to get to her.

"You'll need your strength."

The frustration is mounting. I'm aching to feel her and smell her hair. We're literally separated by bars.

"Fuck me, I need out of this cell." I tear open the turkey jerky and take a long pull, while she dips her delicate hand into a bag of salt and vinegar chips.

"Soon. And you're pretty incredible too. Downright dreamy, really."

"Then let's not wake up." I retake her hand, and she slants her head to get a better view of me through the bars. Her hair flops over her eye, and it's killing me that I can't touch it.

❧ 22 ❧

SABRINA

The moment the cell slides open, his hands frame my face and his tongue is sliding against mine. We've been at the station way too long, it's nearly two in the morning. But my night is far from over. I need to be with this man in every possible way until I leave for the airport at six. I wrap my arms around his neck, and we kiss as if he's been off serving our country or actually in jail for years. There's desperation from our slight separation. His hands settle on my hips, and he murmurs against my lips, "God, you taste good. I missed this."

Such an odd thought, but I missed him too. My tongue is frantic, trying to move into his mouth permanently and searching for a place to take up residence. My tongue is mentally packing boxes and picking out a new couch. He's volleying with mine, then his hands curl around to the top of my ass, and he pulls me closer. I feel his erection, then the nice policeman clears his throat. I jump back from him, and everyone clearly feels awkward.

I tuck my hair behind my ears. I have severe pussy ache now, so I do a couple of lopsided laps around the small room to calm myself down while he handles his paperwork.

WE STEP OUT INTO THE COLD, AND I SAY, "HOW DOES freedom taste?"

He turns and scoops me to him. "Like I need to taste you as soon as humanly fucking possible."

I peck his lips. "Seems like a good plan, and I know just the bed. Come with me." And then, as if on cue, a horse and carriage pull up. I look around, and he's as skeptical as I am.

The driver bellows, "Yo. Yo. You Sabrina?" I don't say a word. "Are you Sabrina Faire and Patrick Donovan?"

We walk hand in hand towards him. He says, "Yes. What's going on here?"

"I'm here to take yous on a ride. I should be fucking sleeping so get in. I'm doing a big ask for my, let's call him, uh, a cousin."

Patrick shrugs and climbs up, pulling me with him. I nestle under the big fuzzy blanket.

"Where yous headed?"

I answer before Patrick can. "The Plaza, please." His head whips around as he glides under the blanket. "It's a long story but my sister got me this baller suite for tonight."

Patrick laughs. "For Ricky?" I laugh too.

"So how do yous know my bookie, I mean cousin, Ricky?"

Patrick says, "Wait. Ricky arranged this?"

"Yeah, he felt bad for his hot head. Said he don't want nothing to do with the cops and wanted to smooth things out with yous two, so everything stays buried."

I blurt, "How the fuck does my sister know Ricky?"

Patrick laughs. "Tell Ricky thanks. We're ready to go. Thanks, man."

I snuggle into him as a chilly New York passes around us, but all I hear are the clip-clop of the horse and his heartbeat. He kisses the top of my head, and I feel a bit like a displaced Hallmark movie. My thoughts aren't closed door, but this is wildly romantic.

23

PATRICK

It's two in the morning and the door is barely closed when I whip off my jacket and coat and throw them on the floor. She's taking hers off in a panic as well. I need closer. I need naked. I need to let my cock do what I promised him all night. Her body slams into mine. She goes for my belt buckle, and I hike up her skirt. My hands reach into her thong at the exact moment her delicate fingers wrap themselves around my cock. We both groan.

"Now," she rasps at me. She unbuttons my shirt. I loosen my tie and whip both over my head. Her hands rake down my chest. I pull her dress down, exposing her bra, and get the full view of this matching set. Fuck me. I thrust my hand back into her thong and feel for her swollen and wanting slit. I grind my palm into her clit, and she moans.

"Make that noise again. Fucking do it again." I slide my fingers down and thrust into her, and she moans loudly.

"Fuck naked. Fuck me now." I claw her dress off, and it falls to the ground. I hook my fingers into her thong. She stares at me as I rip it from her body. She gasps and reaches for the pharmacy bag. She pulls out a tiny fuzzy bear and hurls it into the other room, then finds the box of condoms. I get down on one knee and place a kiss on the most perfect pussy I've ever had the privilege to pucker. Alliteration is a DJ's curse.

I hold her open and lick her. Her hands pull at my hair. I can't take it.

"Run. Go. Scurry to the bed or I'm fucking you against this door."

She squeals and takes off, and the sight of her perfect ass is seared into my brain. I arrive at the door as she turns around. I drop my boxers and fist my cock. I fuck into my hand a couple of times, and her hands tear her bra away.

"They're everything I dreamed of in prison."

She smiles but doesn't laugh. Her hand skitters across my chest and below. I shudder. I say, "And that's it. I know we're hungry but I need you now." And for the third time tonight I pick her up, but this time I throw her on the bed and pull her legs wide. "Fucking gorgeous." She licks her lips and hands me a condom. She watches as if there will be a test later as I roll it on.

I lie on top of her and kiss her roughly. Her hands reach down and guide me home. As I begin to push into her, she arches her back and moans.

Her voice is breathy and her eyes are way too serious. "Patrick."

I match her tone and the moment. "Sabrina." I never want to stop being inside this woman. We lie, basking in the revelation of how perfectly we fit.

24

SABRINA

I'm so tired, and I know he is as well, but we're not sleeping. We're face to face on the pillows. I woke after a forty-five-minute nap to stare at him. Finally, I had to touch his face. The room is gorgeous and decadent, but it's his face I wanted to see, not the room. I'm days away from being thirty, and it's abundantly clear to me, I've never been in love. I thought I had. And I know rationally this can't be it. This is really fucking good lust and infatuation. But it feels unfinished. I can't push that feeling down far enough. *You're not done. The two of you aren't done.* It's invasive like an earworm of "What's New Pussy Cat."

I don't like people; they disappoint you, but this man actually caught fire to be with me. I have an insistent need to know all of him, so when I file him away later today, I'll be able to pull out all the pieces and play with them in the future. I know this is just a moment and I have to go back to my life of Bree in a couple of hours. But from the airport confab to here, it's all been like a wacky and sometimes scary movie. I didn't dislike any of these people. Even poor Ricky Schlong had his moments. It's been a break from my regularly scheduled program. I'm not good at dating, but I am good at him.

So, I ask. I don't overthink. I don't temper who I am to trick him into liking me. He already does. I wish I lived here. Then maybe, just maybe, this night wouldn't be an expiration date.

I put my hand on his cheek, and he turns his head slightly and kisses my palm. I slide it down his arm and settle on his hip.

"What happened?" I ask.

He asks in his smooth as silk voice—it's deep and rich and plays any room he's in like a violin—"What do you mean?"

"I'm not sure how you let me in, but you have. Why do you push everyone away?"

He crooks an eyebrow. "How do I do that?"

"That eyebrow is part of it. Fess up."

I grin, and he leans forward and kisses me, sweet and quick. My body feels like it just sipped hot chocolate on a snowy day. He says, "I'm very charming and most people like me, so I'm confused here, beautiful Sabrina."

"That. That's the thing you do to other people but not to me." I pull the sheet up, but he slips it back down. His hands caress my nipples, then tweak them. I gasp and moan. Then I jab his chest.

He says, "That what? Worship perfect tits?" His hand is caressing my hip and thigh.

"Like bullets bouncing off Superman's "S"—you deflect. You're charming and sexy, but you're also interesting, deep, and emotional. I saw you give our vending leftovers to that homeless man in the police station lobby. I saw you. I see you."

"Why can't you just be great sex? Why can't you be simple?" He removes his hand, and I know what that means.

"Not the first time someone's said that." I sigh and cover up, knowing once again, I fucked it all up. "You're going to leave now, right?"

He grasps my hair between his fingers, moves his hand to the back of my neck and pulls me closer to his face. His eyes are bright with possibility and sincerity. They're vulnerable, like a child, and I want to wrap him up and protect him from his past. I want to pull on my own Superman spandex and keep him safe. But no one lets me do that.

"Quite the opposite." My eyes widen in surprise, and he grins. "I'm not done with you."

"Yet."

I see him flinch a touch. I think we might both try to ruin things before someone else does.

He points at me and says, "You said that, not me." I gasp as my voice and breath elude me. "Humor and deflecting can go a long way in saving the soul of a kid. Don't knock them—like recognizes like—you do it too. I see you, too, beautiful Sabrina. You tell me your ugly and I'll tell you mine." His smile turns a little sad, but he waggles his eyebrows at me, and I melt a little more.

It comes out very unexpectedly. Perhaps because they're the secrets told in the Valentine's vacuum of a one-night stand. "No one has ever seen me. Not my parents or my sisters. I had to barrel through, be tougher, be funnier and faster to be heard or noticed. Or shrink down so they could shine. It worked, but then I couldn't pull it back. I couldn't be as soft and vulnerable as men in my past wanted, or as bold to be a partner. I couldn't lay down my sword. Or be as agreeable as they'd like. The snark got me in trouble in school, with men, and at work. I've lost jobs because of it too."

I smile as he says, "Idiots. Thank god they didn't see you, so I could."

He kisses me, taking my mouth as if it was always waiting for him. Maybe I have been waiting for him. Our tongues skip and dance, and just as things start to get heated again, I pull away. I always pull away when things get too much. I'm shocked I was able to orgasm so many times with him. Usually I can't and fake it. Usually I can't let go unless it's by myself. I'm afraid it's too much.

He sighs. "Funny brings you friends. Sarcasm bonds you to people fast. I was always the new kid, so I never got too close to people because they were interchangeable. I'd be gone soon enough, so I left them laughing. If I wanted to, I could attend seven different high school reunions. My father wasn't a good man but an ok con man. I feel as if I need to pay his karmic debt. I give back whenever I can. Tonight's leftovers were a small thing I try to always do."

He's good. He's good in bed. He's good with me, and his heart is plain good.

"And your mother?"

"Surviving and avoiding. She has a life in Minnesota that appears stable and secure. I only wish she'd been strong enough to give that to me and my brothers. She took it for herself and in the process taught all three of us to look out for ourselves any way we could."

"She left your grifter dad?"

He flicks my nose. I smile, then curl my arm around him. I kiss his hand.

"She left all of us. She's made amends since and is some kind of zombie cheerleader in our lives now. But we can't forget those five years. She left us with him and his traveling con man carnival that showed us most of America and taught us the art of disappearing into the night. He dealt in fake phone cards, credit cards, and banking schemes. Just before we skipped town, he'd pull his harried-office-man patented scam on one of those check cashing places. Sometimes he'd hit two or three of them in an hour. He'd pocket the money and we'd be gone before the checks bounced. To his credit, he didn't leave us and always made sure we were fed and enrolled in school in the next town. I'm a little shocked I didn't end up with rickets from eating hot dogs for almost a year straight. I probably still glow in the dark from the nitrates."

"Is he still a criminal?"

"No. He's gone. But ironically, I'm the only one to end up in the slammer."

He jokes, and I don't want this moment to get deflected as well.

I climb on top of him, and his hands go to my ass. He caresses lightly, and I lean down and lick his lips. Then he grabs two handfuls, and I really want him.

I say, "Kiss me. Be with me. Not one of them deserves to be in this room with us tonight. None of our family. Just us. Kiss me, Ricky. Shit. I mean Patrick." He laughs and lifts his head to meet mine. Those slightly swollen and luscious lips feel so good as I press my body to his. My nipples brush against the hard planes of his chest and instantly peak. I feel him grow, too, as he squeezes my ass and adjusts himself underneath me. He scoots me just a touch forward, and I grind into him.

He groans. "Fuck, Melanie, that's so good." I laugh on his lips, and we both burst into silly giggles. I shake my head and move a little bit.

"Thank you for telling me."

"You're welcome. I don't know why I did. Oh, wait, it was to get you to grind down on my cock again." His grip on my ass is commanding and robust, as he directs me right back to where he wants me. I surrender. The last shreds of my confusion over this nutty evening fall away as I reach behind him for another condom. I rock on his hard cock for a moment, then sit up. I scoot down his legs and suck on the crown, and he moans louder. I flat tongue him from the shaft up and down again, then take him deep into my mouth, hollowing out my cheeks. His hips move, and I breathe through my nose as I take him down. He thrusts into my mouth, and I look up at him. He's lost in ecstasy, then opens his eyes and sees me.

"So, fucking ridiculously otherworldly beautiful."

I pop him out of my mouth. "Me or your cock?"

He laughs. "Very funny. Put my dick back in your mouth, woman." I nod, and without warning, I deep throat him again while squeezing his balls. There's a guttural noise, similar to the sound he made before he came before.

"Nope. I had a very filling dinner of Snickers and salt and vinegar chips, and I couldn't possibly swallow another thing."

He flips me over and pins me to the bed in one motion. Then he runs his hands up my arms, placing them over my head. He plucks the condom from my hand.

"I guess I have to cancel the room service spread." He settles between my legs, staring at me as his fingers open me up. He circles my clit with his finger followed by his tongue. I moan, then he's gone. He's kneeling but still holding me open, exposing my sensitive bud to the air.

He says, "But what are we going to do instead? All I really had planned was snacking. I love a good club sandwich. Hmm. Let me think." He strokes himself, then taps his hard dick on my amped-up clit as if he's tapping his finger on his chin, trying to come up with an idea. He looks off to the side as if he's contemplating something and keeps tapping. It's driving me wild.

He says, "It's a real head-scratcher. What can we do to fill the rest of our time together?" Tap. Tap. Tap. "Board games are out. I don't play chess, and I've seen everything on Netflix already, so I guess, we're just going to have to dirty fuck each other until dawn. Unless you can think of something." He looks at me but keeps tapping his dick on to my clit.

I'm on fire now. My clit anticipates each tap and gets more sensitive with each pass. I arch into him, searching for more contact, but he won't touch me except for the tap tap tap of his insanely hard cock.

I shrug and lift my pelvis to meet the tap. Then, I say, "I can't. I'm no good at Sudoku or word play."

"A movie?"

"Hate movies." I groan. Tap. Tap. Tap.

He offers up, "We could catch up on our correspondence?"

I say, "I'll lick the stamps." He flicks my pointed nipple. I gasp. Holy fuck, I'm hot for him.

"No, silly. Do they even make lickable stamps anymore?"

I can't take anymore, and I yell, "Oh GOOD GOD. Just fuck me right now." He grins and rolls the condom on in two seconds. He swipes up the wetness that's gathered and smears it on my clit as he pushes inside.

"Now, there's a good idea."

He rolls his hips, and I rise to meet him. With each crest we increase our volume and speed. He pistons in and out of me. I'm so fucking ready. I clutch his biceps. He reaches between us, and I'm gone. I scream, "Patrick. Oh. God. Fuck. Patrick. Patrick. Yes. Yes." His grip and the orgasm have a firm hold on me. I freeze, then release everything with a shudder.

"Christ you're hot when you come. Now do me? Am I hot when I come?" I can't laugh or smile. I'm still not back in my body, as he doubles down and touches the deepest part of me. Fuck, he's so deep. I begin to contract around him again just as he comes hard, making unintelligible sounds, and I'm right there with him. Moaning, groaning, and coming in a torrent of expletives and feelings.

He leaps up to dispose of the condom then he's on top of me as we catch our breath. The feelings are still rippling over my skin. I kiss his cheek and say, "Yes. You are that hot when you come."

❦ 25 ❦

PATRICK

I wake in a panic. It's 5:31 in the morning. We only fell asleep an hour ago. She's snoring. Full-on, mouth open, snoring. I wish I could say it turned me off. I shake her, but she doesn't wake. I check her breathing. I have no choice. It's fucking ripping me up, but I'm already late. I have to catch the ride that's picking me up in twenty minutes. This is an impossible situation. I have to get home. I want to pull her to me, shove her in my pocket, and take her with me, but I don't even know what that looks like. I don't have time to explain. I don't know what life will look like, I do know that my life will be different after this Valentine's disastrous perfect evening.

I can't find a pen anywhere. And she won't wake up. I want her to call me. I run into the bathroom and scribble a note on the mirror. I leave my number. I forgot to ask for hers. I know her last name. I would Google her if my phone weren't dead. I let the door close. I hope it's enough of an explanation that she realizes I'm shitty with time management and not a dick. I will track her down today. Or later, after a fucking nap. And some aloe on my Achilles cigarette burn. I want to send her arnica for her bruise. That's stupid. Fuck. I have to go. I have to sort out if this was real. I take off running so I'm not late. This is harder and probably easier. It's up to her now.

It's frigid outside. But Sabrina has left me so warm and fucking mushy inside I don't even feel my lack of gloves. I only feel her. I only hope when I figure out what to do about this ridic woman, she'll listen to why.

❧ 26 ❧

SABRINA

I wake up in a seriously sticky puddle of my own drool. It's gross, but it's also jarring as my 6:15 a.m. wake-up call is going off. I felt like I just went to sleep. Fuck. Wait. Shit. I sit up and look around. I sleep like the dead; I didn't hear him wake up. Hopefully I didn't drool on him.

"Patrick? Where are you?" There are noises in the bathroom. I check the clock. I'm not sure I even have time for a quickie. I have to hurry to the airport.

I fling open the bathroom door and spread my arms on the doorframe, so he gets a full view of my body. There's screaming and yelling prayers to Jesus.

"AHHHHHH. I KNOCKED. I KNOCKED. Jesus, help me. Jesus, take the wheel! But no one answered."

"What the fuck?" I scramble for the closest towel and it's a hand towel. I choose to cover my naked lower bits and drape my hand across my boobs.

"Miss. Miss. Room was empty."

"I'm so sorry." She's in the middle of cleaning the mirror, and there are red streaks on her rag. I look up and scream.

"STOP CLEANING. Please stop." There's a note blazing before me on the mirror in lipstick, but she's already cleaned part of it. My heart leaps in excitement, then plummets.

I grab the rag from her, turning it over and over as if the rest of the note would be preserved in the Windex smears like a silly putty on a cartoon strip. Shit. Shit. And now my boobs are in her face. She wincing and trying to look away.

"I'm so sorry to scare you, please go." She runs from the bathroom, and I sit on the edge of the bathtub staring at my note. The one I could only dream of but now is nothing. I know his last name. How many Patrick Donavan's work for Sirius? Or perhaps this is fate telling me not to force things. This is the universe setting things the way they're supposed to be. I stare at the mirror. I never even told him I don't live in New York.

> *Sexpot – Gorgeous, Beautiful Sabrina*
> *We're not don—*

The rest of the message is smeared beyond recognition. It's gone. I laugh uncontrollably. The only part of Patrick that's still left written on the mirror is *Rick*.

I dig my phone from my coat and snap a picture of the message. So I can remember he thought we could be something. That kind of shit never works out for me. I'm always the one invited along to make an even number for a reservation. He made me feel special. We were the odd ones that fit together to make a whole. And not a Tinywhole. A whole thing. I sigh, throw my hair up, and dash to the airport.

. . .

THIS FUCKING FLIGHT IS SO FREAKING EARLY.

"United flight to Chicago, out of JFK, right?"

I nod and think about the shoes I left behind. I didn't need some twisted memento of the best night/worst morning of my life. I watch as Patrick fades along with the New York skyline. I wonder where he is in this vast city. I know Chicago is a huge city, but it always feels manageable versus the chaos of Manhattan. Manhattan suits him. I could open my phone and find him right now but I'm not sure he wants to hear from me. I mean he's got to be on social media but he didn't even leave a number. Or what if he did and the traumatized cleaning woman has it. Like she wrote it down and she's going to call him. She might have blurred that part of the message first because she's working with the universe to conspire against me. I'll bet she'll call, she's braver than me. I can't call. Maybe when I'm not so freaking tired I'll stalk him. But that would be so awkward. I already have too much of that in my life. This feels like a heartbreak, and it was only one night. I swipe a tear. I'm so fucking confused. I'm tired. Even if we did connect somehow, I don't know if I'm built for a long-distance relationship.

Here's a dreadful thought: what if I'm only built for him.

I TRUDGE ONTO THE PLANE. I'M A HOT MESS OF SWEATS AND a disheveled bun. I splashed water on my face, but it didn't take. I'm clammy from running and almost missing my flight. I shove my bag in the overhead and nod to the person in the window seat as I take my place on the aisle. I swear I can still smell the man. His outdoorsy cedary musk is wafting through the cabin. Or am I having a psychotic break? Time will tell.

Our takeoff is delayed, and we're tarmac stranded. I turn my phone on. The one that doesn't have his number. I should probably tell my sister Ricky is a criminal, or maybe she knows. I have a million texts and notifications. The airport squad's been texting.

TABI: Well, she's dead. I liked her. It's a shame. Rory, would you like to say a few words?

I keep scrolling through and laughing at their messages. Seems Ben had quite the night. They all seem bold enough to own their emotions. Even Rory, the stoic, sexy, Scot seems head over heels for his Zoe. They're brave enough. I hope I will be someday.

I'm a bit nauseous without real food for almost fifteen hours and a bit sad that the universe and the mortified maid are determined to keep me lonely. My eyes tear up again at the thought of his perfect face, and it stabs my heart. I shake it off. I'll cry later in the privacy of my own closet. I throw my head onto the tray table. Despite the bruises, the arrest record, the broken shoes, starvation, fire, swelling hives, and abandonment, it was the best night of my life. He really did see me and like me. It's going to take a minute to get over this night, but maybe there's someone in Chicago who can make me feel like he did.

Or, what's more likely, I'm doomed by fate to rot on my couch while trying to recreate my prison picnic every February 14th to stir up some emotion resembling what's overwhelming me right now. I know time will take the enthusiasm and the minutiae of tonight, but I hope I can hold on to the feeling—at least a little. But no, it's all going to be loneliness and many group lunches as the elderly single gal for me. I know I'm just about to be thirty, and everyone says there's time to meet the "one." But I did, and I only got to keep him for ten hours.

I feel the flight attendant before he gets close. I wave my hand at him without looking up from the crook of my arm. "Nothing for me. Nothing ever again will be good. Nothing.

Not a beverage or a snack I have to purchase because nothing is free in this life. There's nothing you can do. So no thank you, life." He huffs, then slides a piece of paper under my arm.

I open it and see the opening sentence, then I lean into the aisle frantically, looking up and down.

> *My dearest Melanie,*
> *Breakfast at my place? Seat 2B.*
> *Forever yours,*
> *Ricky*

I grin and claw at my seatbelt. It won't unhook, and I grunt and curse. The dude at the window looks at me.

He turns, red-faced. "You can't get up. You'll delay the plane. Where are you going?"

The flight attendant leans over and puts his finger up to his mouth then turns back to me. "He paid for you to move."

I smile and throw my arms in the air. "Destiny. I'm leaping into muthafucking destiny. The universe doesn't hate me! Take care, cranky man from the window seat. And happy day after Valentine's Day."

Running up the aisle, I bang my thigh on a stupid armrest. What's one more bruise? He's in first class, far from the back of the plane. I must have walked right by him. I did smell him. Thank god, I'm not crazy.

I arrive at his seat after dodging a crying baby and surprising an old lady who splashed me with apple juice by accident. He's pretending to read. He looks disheveled with his rushed sexy bed head. There's a small half-moon bruise under his eye. He's gorgeous and perfect and he's here. His skin is slightly flushed from what I hope is excitement. He's wearing a bright green t-shirt stretched across his strong and cut chest. I'm confused. It's a shirt from a bar in my old neighborhood. I say nothing, but my heart, vagina, and mind are buzzing with excitement and joy. I'm not sure I even knew what joy really felt like, but here it is. I stare straight ahead, playing his game. I put my arm on my armrest next to his. There's a heat coming off us as our arms almost touch. But yet, it all feels totally normal. Like we've flown together a thousand times. It's like we get to skip the parts of a relationship that neither of us likes or are any good at. He laces his fingers through mine. And we fit. I look at our hands and catch his eyes.

I narrow my eyes as I entwine my fingers in his. I wait as he captures my hand and heart. I even out my breath and eventually say, "First class? You owe me more than a bag of chips." He kisses the top of my hand.

"I told you we weren't done. How about the drink I never got to buy you last night? Does that work for you, beautiful Sabrina?" The flight attendant delivers mimosas to us.

I'm awash in that pesky joy from his compliment. It's a surge of something more than lust. I don't know what to do with it; it's oozing out of me without a place to put it.

His voice is quiet. "I checked my phone a thousand times this morning. I missed you but apparently, I didn't even warrant a text. I get it, your busy schedule of getting up and to the airport, couldn't even find a second."

I quickly explain, "I didn't know you left a number. The maid cleaned most of the message before I could get it."

"Likely excuse. Wait, she came in while you were sleeping?" He cocks his head to the side.

"Why didn't you wake me? You left me."

He laughs at my vulnerability and takes both of my hands in his. "I tried. I even checked to see if you were breathing after I shook you for like two minutes and you didn't wake."

I exhale. "Yeah, I sleep crazy deep. Should have told you that."

He smirks. "You think? Freaked me the fuck out."

I shift to get closer to him. "Freaked the maid the fuck out too. She bolted after getting a good look at the hickeys on my stomach and my full beaver, yelling, 'But I knocked. I knocked.'"

He laughs. "I was going to miss my ride to the airport so I had to bolt. Hence the lipstick number. But make no mistake, you are absolutely not a mistake." I grin as he leans forward, and our lips are so close. The recycled air is buzzing between us, then we come together and kiss gently. It's quiet and perfect. I grin into it, and he pulls back. He runs his knuckle along my jaw. I sigh.

He says reverently, "And how long will I have you in my town?" I sit up, and our hands break apart. He looks disturbed. I gesture with my mimosa at him. I swallow the drink in two sips. My hands are instantly a little damp, and I don't want to have shattered glassware while I ask what the hell he means. Given our twelve-hour history, one of us is getting a scratched cornea if that happens. That sweet dopamine high is gone, and now I'm sizzling with adrenaline. I lean over, grab at his shirt, and yank him as close as possible. This can't be real. He can't really fucking be real.

"YOUR TOWN?"

He crooks that sexy as hell eyebrow at me. He looks thoroughly confused. He's not nearly as confused as I am. "Yes, as in Chicago—'My Kind of Town.'"

I cannot contain myself. "As in 'Sweet Home Chicago?'" My voice is loud, the pitch is about four tones above my normal speaking voice.

He nods at me, still confused.

"I don't need Christmas or my birthday. I don't need any other holiday ever again because this is the biggest holiday gift of my life on February 15th. From now on, we'll celebrate

Destiny Day going forth, and that's it." I grin widely. "Clark and Balmoral." My heart flips as I tell him my cross streets.

There's a small gasp. He squeezes his eyes shut, shakes his head in disbelief, and smiles. He leans forward and says, "Wisconsin and Sedgwick."

I whisper his neighborhood, "Old Town." His lips brush over mine, and I kiss him. And nothing else matters.

He hovers over my lips and whispers the name of my neighborhood, "Andersonville. You don't live in New York." It's a statement, not a question.

I whisper back, "Neither do you."

He shakes his head at me. "Thank god. I had no desire to figure out how to commuter-plane date you."

My eyes light up, and I bite my bottom lip. "You want to date me?"

"I want to do a lot of things to you but I'll start with dating."

His hand tangles into my hair as he pulls me as close as possible. I'd like to climb on top of him, but I'm a little sore and tired. Gymnastics might result in a hospital visit for us. I back off and shake my head, but he doesn't let me go far.

I say, in between light kisses on my neck, "Well, I guess we ended up in a long-distance relationship anyway."

He smiles. "So far. Fifteen minutes and six neighborhoods away." I shrug as if it's an impossible task. He flashes the smile that arrested me last night before we even spoke. I wonder if it was meant for me all along. "We should probably start saving to meet up soon. I guess we could plan a weekend together somewhere in the middle."

"A weekend in Wrigleyville. Sounds heavenly but only if the Clark 22 bus is running on time."

His thumb strokes my lip gently then tugs. "I have faith we can survive a little adversity. I mean, I literally burned for you."

We kiss deep and long. Our tongues find the answers to all the questions. They're dipping into our future, forging our new path. The one we get to explore together.

He says, "Now, if you don't mind, I had a hell of a night and I'm exhausted." I giggle, as he throws a blanket over me and arranges one for himself. He slides my hand into his. "So, quit your yapping and sleep with me. Then later, I can ask all the questions we forgot. Like what's your favorite pizza topping, and which side of my bed will you sleep on?" I laugh and so does he. There's an ease to it.

I put my head on his shoulder. We breathe in and out, but the excitement of knowing this isn't the end, it's the beginning, keeps us from passing out.

"Hey, Sabrina," he whispers into my hair.

"Yes, Patrick."

"Wanna have dinner tonight? I could make a reservation."

I grin. "Can't. Having dinner with Ricky."

He tips my head up to face his, then he puts my forehead to his. He kisses me quickly, and I grin. "Tell him, you're taken."

I've never wanted to be someone's before. But I'm already his.

"Hmm, I am?"

He says, "You are. Where else am I going to find someone who's so safe?"

"Safe?" I don't want to be safe. I'm done being safe. I'm bold now. My face sags a touch.

He lifts my chin. "After what we've endured, we're disaster proof."

I smile and sigh. "Disaster proof."

THE END.

EPILOGUE

TABI: *Are you dead? Seriously. Tell me. Are you forever changed by the blind date? Is it a horror show?*

SABRINA: *Not dead. Not horror. But yes, forever changed. Tell you later. Eating dinner with the hot man from last night. He lives here in Chicago. Ben, did you figure out how to find her?*

BEN: *NO. And if I can chime in here for a moment, certainly glad you're not dead. But I have an issue. I'm forever changed from Valentine's Day as well but don't have a handle on the situation. She's perfect.*

RORY: *If it's love, no one ever does.*

BEN: *Thanks, mate. I needed to hear that.*

TABI: *Fuck me. Wise advice from our resident Jock.*

RORY: *Did you Google ways to insult me as a Scot?*

RORY: *Hi! I stole his phone. Hi. I don't know you, Tabi, but, hi. Hi, everyone. I'm Rory's. Well, I'm Rory's Zoe. Tabitha, please keep needling him. I get loads of joy from the smoke spilling out of his ears when he reads a text from you.*

RORY: *Disregard the redhead.*

TABI: *Hi, Zoe! Greek? I'm Tabitha Meira Costas Aganos. I have a shit ton of cousins named Zoe.*

RORY: DISREGARD THE REDHEAD.

JONATHAN: Can we get back to Sabrina before we get to Ben's issue? Love on the horizon?

TABI: Jonathan, did you get laid? Dry Spell over?

JONATHAN: I do not want to talk about it.

TRISTAN: No need mate. Now, Sabrina, dear, are you changed for the better?

SABRINA: We'll see. But so far, absofuckinglutely. Ben, believe in destiny. I didn't and I was an idiot. Talk to you later. Good luck Ben.

TRISTAN: Now that Sabrina is sorted and I have faith Ben will find her one way or another. What do I do about the woman I'm in love with and I've never seen her legs?

THE END. FOR NOW...

THANK YOU!!! THANK YOU SO MUCH FOR READING OUR little lark!

EVIE AND KELLY'S HOLIDAY DISASTERS WILL CONTINUE with Cookout Carnage for the Fourth of July. Tristan and Jonathan will both work to get their Happily Ever Afters.

AND COMING NOVEMBER 18TH, EVIE AND KELLY'S HOLIDAYS Disasters will bring you Christmas Chaos with Rory and Zoe from the Kinloch series and Tabi and Bax from the Five Families Vineyard series.

Pre-order Cookout Carnage at mybook.to/CookoutCarnage

Pre-order Christmas Chaos at mybook.to/ChristmasChaos

IF YOU ENJOYED CUPID CALAMITY, PLEASE WRITE US A couple of lines reviewing it on Amazon, Goodreads and Bookbub. It's so easy and your reviews mean everything to us!

HAPPY VALENTINE'S DAY OR DESTINY DAY, FOR THOSE WHO celebrate.

ALSO BY EVIE ALEXANDER & KELLY KAY

Evie & Kelly's Holiday Disasters

Volume One

Cupid Calamity

3rd February 2022

Cookout Carnage

6th June 2022

Christmas Chaos

18th November 2022

ABOUT EVIE ALEXANDER

Evie Alexander is the author of sexy romantic comedies with a very British sense of humour. She takes a method approach to her work, believing her capacity to repeatedly fail at life and love is what has given her such a rich supply of material for her writing. Her interests include reading, eating, saving the world, and fantasizing about people who only exist between the pages of her books. She lives in the West Country with her family.

Also by Evie Alexander
Full-length Romantic Comedy Novels

THE KINLOCH SERIES

Highland Games

Hollywood Games

Kissing Games

Musical Games

Evie's website and newsletter sign up:
www.eviealexanderauthor.com

Goodreads:
bit.ly/eviegoodreads

instagram.com/eviealexanderauthor

bookbub.com/authors/evie-alexander

facebook.com/eviealexanderauthor

twitter.com/Evie_author

pinterest.com/eviealexanderauthor

amazon.com/Evie-Alexander/e/B08ZJGLP29

ABOUT KELLY KAY

Kelly is the author of nine steamy and funny contemporary romance full-length novels with the tenth on its way - Spring 2022. She's a writer, married to a writer, mother of a creative dynamo of a ten-year-old boy in Chicago, and currently looking for either a cup of coffee or a glass of wine.

She's gotten very used to waking up to a Zoom call request from England. And Evie's gotten quite used to seeing Kelly's bedhead and her sucking down copious amounts of coffee as they dreamed up this bonkers project. Time Zones can be a bitch.

Also by Kelly Kay

Full-length Contemporary Romance & Romantic Comedy Novels

FIVE FAMILIES VINEYARD SERIES

LaChappelle/Whittier Vineyard Trilogy
    Crushing
    Rootstock
    Uncorked

Stafýlia Cellars Duet
    Over A Barrel

Under The Bus

Gelbert Family Winery Standalone
Meritage: An Unexpected Blend

CHI TOWN STORIES

Lyrical Duet
Shock Mount
Crossfade

A Predestined Standalone
Present Tense
Spring 2022

STANDALONE BOOKS

Side Piece

Kelly's website and newsletter sign up:
www.kellykayromance.com

https://tinyurl.com/amazonKellyK
facebook.com/groups/kellykaybookblends
https://tinyurl.com/KellyKgoodreads
instagram.com/kelly_kay_books
bookbub.com/profile/kelly-kay

ACKNOWLEDGMENTS

Bloggers, readers, bookstagrammers, alpha and beta readers - there is no book without you. Thank you so much for promoting and caring about our insanity. Trust us, we care about yours too. And our friends who are a constant source of joy and support, thank you.

Our editor, Aimee Walker. We know you were scared when we first told you about the project but we couldn't have pulled it off without you. Thank you. Also, there's more coming. Should we send Prosecco?

> Mike Thomas, there is not no nothing you don't knew about the grammars and words and we is grateful for your guidence.

Margaret Amatt - your enthusiasm to jump on board our crazy train is much appreciated. It's the cover of our dreams. Thank you so much! And Marina, thank you for your wonderful illustrations.

Allison, Becky, Julia, Michael, Pash, Sandie & Tori – thanks for your encouragement and eyeballs on this first set of novellas.

Victoria, Mandy and Taryn at Emlin Press. Well, thank you for everything else. Seriously, EVERYTHING else.

And the husbands. We can't do any of this without your support, love, and overlooking our occasional lapse in house-keeping or decorum. And the 10-year-olds who have to keep popping onto our Zooms to say hello to a stranger. Elway and Charlie, thanks for putting up with your silly mommies.